JASMINE SEA

PHILLIPA NEFRI CLARK

PHILLIPA NEFRI CLARK
Mystery. Love. Suspense.

Jasmine Sea

© 2017 Phillipa Nefri Clark

Further the author acknowledges the use of these brand names: Lotus Elite S, Facebook, Frisbee, Range Rover, Porsche.

Cover design: Steam Power Studios

A QUICK NOTE...

This series is set in Australia and written in Aussie/British English for an authentic experience.

For Ian, Nick, and Alex. Your belief in me keeps me strong. And Maverick.
Always there to help.

1

LEAVING RIVER'S END

"I can't wait another minute!" Martha's eyes sparkled as she reached for Thomas' hand.

"Always impatient." Thomas kissed her fingers. "What will you be like at the airport?"

"I quite like airports. Good place to read. Now where is my ticket?"

"Where it will be safe." He tapped his jacket. "Can't have it falling into the ocean."

"Never let me forget it, will you?"

The words were meant to be under her breath, but she knew Thomas heard. With a grin, he checked his watch. "Hope those two get back before the bus arrives."

Martha bit her lip and he took her hand again. "She'll be here when we return."

"But, what if she isn't? I've only just found her."

"Now, come on. Why wouldn't she stay? She has the cottage and Martin. And really, who would leave Randall?"

"You're leaving him."

"Maybe I shouldn't go."

"Thomas! I'm being serious. What if something happens?"

"It won't. Listen to me. Better yet, turn around."

Hand in hand, Christie and Martin hurried out of a Green Bay shop. Christie said something and Martin burst into laughter.

Thomas put his arm around Martha's shoulders. "Never heard the boy laugh that way until she came along." He glanced behind. "Our ride's arriving."

"Oh, I'm sorry we took so long!" Christie threw her arms around Martha as the bus pulled in. "I wanted you to take this." She held out a box. "It's a small camera. All you need to do is point and shoot."

"I shall miss you, dear!" Martha kissed Christie's cheek, then reached for Martin. "You too, young man."

Martin offered his cheek. "We'll miss you as well."

"What about me?" Thomas demanded.

"What about you?"

"Trying to get rid of me so you keep the dog."

"Randall is already my dog, Granddad."

Passengers alighted from the bus and the driver followed, opening the cavity underneath. Martin and Thomas carried the luggage over and helped stow it.

Martha whispered to Christie. "Stay safe, my darling girl."

"Of course I will!" Christie hugged her great aunt. "Enjoy Ireland, take lots of photos, and when you get home we can work out where you two will be living."

"Have a perfectly fine house in the mountains." Thomas held his arms out for Christie. "That's where my bride and I will be."

"It isn't settled yet!" Martha tapped him on the shoulder. "Come on, old man."

The driver climbed back into the bus. Thomas guided Martha up the steps, his hand on her elbow. They found seats at the front and settled in as the front door closed with a whoosh.

Here they were, beginning their honeymoon. Martha reached for Thomas' hand as the bus left town. The man who had haunted her dreams for a lifetime was finally her husband.

The last time she had been on this road, in this direction, she had been running away – in December, 1967.

Martha had no idea why they had to leave almost before dawn, but Patrick, her father, was insistent. He liked to take his time, to be careful through the hairpins.

She couldn't remember the whole family going to Melbourne together; certainly not since her early childhood. Now, though, her mother Lilian sat beside Patrick, keeping half an eye on his speed. Dorothy dozed beside Martha.

This felt wrong. Every mile took her further away from Thomas. Further away from making up with him. Almost a week ago, in the midst of a violent storm, she had broken their engagement after seeing him with her near-naked best friend. Ex best friend.

His words went round and round her head. "I will wait for you, Martha! Every morning at the end of the jetty."

Their jetty. The one she had slipped off during the storm, into waves which sucked her under and would have claimed her life. But Thomas found her.

Why, oh why, did her pride do this? Make her say things she didn't mean and, even worse, take action like now. This was no simple visit to the city. Martha was staying with Dorothy for a while, until she worked out her future. Lilian was joining them.

"We will spend some lovely time together. Just the three girls seeing what Melbourne has to offer." Lilian had been so excited that Martha allowed herself to be talked into this. After all, it was only for a little while, until Thomas apologised and made everything better.

Now, Martha blinked a few times to clear her vision and reminded herself she was in a much happier part of her life. The bus wound smoothly around those same curves, a vivid blue ocean on one side and saltbush on the other.

"What are you thinking?"

Martha smiled up at Thomas. "I can't wait to show you my little house in Ireland. Introduce you to my friends. It's so pretty you will want to paint all the time."

He squeezed her hand. "Anything else?"

The same engagement ring she'd thrown into the sand during the storm was again on her finger, exactly where it was meant to be. Even if now her hands were aged and her once strong body weakened with each passing year.

Tears brimmed. "So much lost time."

"Then we shall make sure that not another moment is wasted. My beautiful girl, time doesn't matter anyway. Now, tell me more about Ireland."

Christie and Martin waved until the bus was out of sight. As one, they lowered their arms. Martin reached out and pulled Christie in for a cuddle. "They'll be fine."

"Of course they will."

"Thomas is very responsible and careful."

"And Martha is well travelled. She knows airports and passports and all the stuff Thomas doesn't."

"Yes. So you can stop worrying."

Christie leaned back a little to look at Martin. "Me?"

"Well, I'm not worried."

"Right."

"Though I am concerned that pile of junk Thomas drives won't make it back to River's End."

Christie giggled. "No wonder they insisted on catching the bus. I doubt it would have got to Melbourne."

"If you had a sensible car with room for the luggage, we could have driven them all the way."

"Me? What about if you just had a car, instead of a decrepit motor-bike! And don't knock my beautiful Lotus!" She slid her arms around his neck. "You are impossible. But I do love you."

"Which is a good thing, or else you'd be walking home. Insulting my most prized possession."

Christie raised herself on her toes to touch her lips to his. "Anyway, they'll be home in a few weeks. And I've got a cottage to renovate."

Martin took her hand as they walked down the road to where Thomas' old Land Rover was parked. "Thomas is determined they'll live at his place."

"But you've said it is old and run-down now. Surely moving into town will be better for them?"

"Do you think we'll make it back without a stop to cool it down?" Martin opened the passenger door for Christie.

She hopped in. "Shall we make a bet?"

"Nope. Let's just hope for the best." Behind the wheel, Martin turned the key. After a splutter, the motor roared. With a bit of force, he got it into gear and onto the road.

"Did you know that my great-grandfather's grandfather won Palmerston House in a game of poker?" Christie asked.

"A good reason not to gamble."

"Oh, I don't know. Imagine suddenly having a property through nothing more than luck and being in the right place at the right time."

Martin glanced across in amusement. "Yes, imagine."

"You mean the cottage? I guess so. Much as I love it, sometimes it feels like a great weight. You know, all the tragedy around it and now, all the work it needs."

"Anything good about it?"

Christie's face lit up. "Nothing at all. Except bringing me to River's End to meet the love of my life."

Martin squeezed her leg. Now out of Green Bay, the twisting road took his attention and Christie was content to gaze out at the ocean. Never did the powerful majesty of the sea fail to touch her. Some deep, primal part of her soul needed to be near it.

Born in the outback, her first sight of the ocean was at the age of seven from the aeroplane that had brought her to Melbourne after her parents died. She went to the beach at St Kilda for the first time a few months later. Gran forbade her to swim in the sea, her fury terrifying Christie the one and only time she disobeyed.

"You okay?"

"Hmm? Oh, just thinking."

"About me, I hope."

"Kind of. More about the ocean. But if you were in the ocean, I'd be thinking about you."

"Right."

Christie sneaked a glance at him. Dressed in a checked shirt with rolled-up sleeves and his favourite jeans, he was so good-looking that keeping her hands to herself was a struggle. "I didn't know you could drive."

"Why wouldn't I drive?"

"You don't have a car."

"Not a fan of cars."

"Well, you drive really well."

"I probably observe the speed limit and conditions a bit more than you do, young lady."

"To celebrate Martha and Thomas heading to Ireland, shall we go out for dinner?"

"Changing the subject." Martin observed. "Okay. Let's go and toast their honeymoon. Their incredibly overdue honeymoon."

The River's End sign came into view. Martin slowed, indicated, and turned into Christie's street. The old Land Rover complained in the lower gear, but was great for navigating the potholes on the other side of the disused railway line.

In the driveway, Martin let the motor idle. "At the pub tonight?"

"Sounds good. I'll walk down."

Martin leaned over and touched Christie's face. "I love you, sweetheart. Thomas and Martha will have the time of their lives. So, we need to be living ours." He kissed Christie with a sweet tenderness. Heart racing, she closed her eyes and surrendered to the knowledge that she was loved. Absolutely loved.

Trust her judgement.

He turned back toward his own home, high on the opposite cliff. When she returned, they could begin to plan their future.

3

BACK IN DOCKLANDS

Christie stood at the window in her hotel room, one hand on the glass, as she peered down to dark water lapping against timber walkways. Leisure craft dotted the man-made bay. City lights flickered on beyond Etihad Stadium and, from here, Christie saw the apartment she'd lived in until late last year.

No lights shone there. Derek would not be home for hours, if his usual routine still stood. She'd spent three years of her life there – two of them with him. Her furniture, homewares, all her special touches remained, abandoned when she'd left.

The palm of her hand was cold on the glass. She stepped back, rubbing it. Why did this matter? These past months were without doubt the best of her life, and in a few days she'd be home again.

———

Familiar city sounds woke Christie before dawn. Trains in the distance. Traffic. The boats. A siren. She watched the sky lighten from her bed. Her view at home was to the same sky but through old trees.

Less than an hour later, pulling her make-up case along behind, she hurried through the almost deserted shopping precinct of

Ray darted to Christie's other side. "Ah, I see what you're doing. Excellent distraction. Now, you never did tell us about being at your worst."

"No, I didn't."

"So?"

"So, there's my hotel."

"Shall we come up for a drink and you can fill us in?" Ray persisted. Christie stopped and threw her arms around him.

"I love you."

He squeezed her back. "Not even one drink?"

"Not even one!"

With a laugh, she shooed them back to their own building. Her smile faded.

I'll miss you so much.

Her life was split in two

Outside her hotel, Christie stopped to squeeze rain from her hair.

A taxi drove past, abruptly stopping at the curb a few metres further along. Christie glanced across at the movement, but nobody got out.

She'd had enough of the rain and wanted a quick hot shower, another glass of wine, and a long conversation with Martin.

The moment Christie entered the hotel, the passenger door opened. A deluge began, soaking the man who stood on the pavement even after the taxi drove away. Derek Hobbs stared at the hotel. Through the window, he saw Christie head for the elevators.

She was out of sight. Derek hurried to the windows, darting from one to another until he saw her again. She stepped into the elevator and glanced his way after pressing the button. He froze. The doors closed and Christie was gone. Again.

4

IMAGINING THE WORST

Top down, the Lotus rounded the last curve before home. Christie pulled over to a shoulder, as she had done on the first time she'd come here. Then it had been for Gran's funeral, knowing nobody and expecting to leave within a day.

One day turned into a week. Going back to Melbourne – to her life with Derek – was not her first choice by then. The town and her inherited cottage grew on her so fast it was as if she was meant to be here.

Back to her life she had gone though, until Derek showed his narcissistic personality one time too many and brought another woman into their relationship. Not that she knew if he had feelings for Ingrid Kauffman, other than their kindred love of property development, but Christie deserved better.

It was early evening and at the bottom of the hill the town was a picture, with the slow river winding through a break in the cliffs, meeting the sea as a shallow lagoon. The air was oh-so-salty and pure, as a breeze filled Christie's senses.

She loved the city. Loved the movement and life, the restaurants and people. Martin used to call her 'city girl' and in those respects he was right. But River's End held her heart now.

All of a sudden, she had to see Martin. Instead of going home first, she nosed the Lotus back onto the road and past the turn-off to the cottage.

———————

Nobody was there. The sliding door was uncharacteristically closed – locked, in fact. Christie peered through the glass to an uninhabited house. She checked the shed. The old motorbike and the surfboards were present. The studio was as deserted.

The sun almost touched the horizon and hunger gnawed at her stomach. She checked her phone, just in case. No missed calls. No messages. Unlike Martin.

Derek had never bothered letting her know where he was. Annoyed that he'd crossed her mind, Christie pushed the thought away.

———————

By the time she turned the Lotus into the driveway, Christie was so tired that she just wanted to eat and then climb into bed. Even her suitcase could stay in the car overnight. Only her handbag and make-up case made it onto the porch with her.

About to slip the key into the lock, Christie heard a noise from inside and stopped. Heart racing, she stepped back.

The noise again – a small thud against the door. Another step back. Derek had got into the cottage before. But it couldn't be him!

The door handle turned, just a little. Christie eyes widened. The key clanged on the porch as she dropped it, hand flying to her mouth.

"Randall, you need to move out the way if I'm to let Christie in."

The door opened enough for Randall, tail wagging furiously, to rush to Christie. Martin pushed the door completely open with a wide, welcoming smile.

"Wondered where you got to when we heard you drive past."

In spite of the dog circling her in excitement, Christie's hand still covered her mouth. It was Martin and Randall. Not some intruder.

Not Derek.

"Christie?"

"I... I thought..."

Martin reached out for Christie. She rushed into his arms and burst into sobs.

"I thought we'd got past this crying stuff." Martin held a box of tissues for Christie, who sat at the table with Randall beside her.

"Me too. Sorry." She dabbed at her eyes.

Squatting down in front of Christie, Martin cupped her cheek. "I didn't mean to scare you."

She leaned into his hand, fear evaporating with his touch. Her heartbeat was normal again and she was cross about overreacting. Who else would be here? He had a key.

"You okay?"

"I went to your house."

"Ah. We heard you drive past. Thought you must have needed something at the shop."

"No. Just you." Her voice was tiny.

He dropped his hand onto hers and squeezed it. "Come and see your room."

Martin led her down the hallway. The dining room door was closed and Martin tugged at her hand when she hesitated.

At the bedroom door, Martin guided Christie in first. She stopped in awe. The plastering and painting was complete, with the lovely old ceiling rose returned to its position around the new light fitting.

Heavy, sea-blue curtains framed a sparkling new window, with lace curtains draped to one side. Perfect against the pale cream walls.

"I thought you said the painting wouldn't be done yet?"

"It needed doing."

Christie put her arms around Martin's neck and kissed him. "Thank you. No abstract mural?"

He grinned. "Hungry?" Without waiting for an answer, he left. Curious, Christie followed him to the dining room. The minute the door opened, mouth-watering smells of roast chicken wafted out.

On the floor, a colourful blanket was spread out. A picnic basket overflowed with bread sticks, salads, cheeses and chicken pieces. Candles flickered on the windowsill. The two straight-backed chairs – the only furniture in the room – served to hold plates and napkins. An ice bucket, complete with a bottle of Chardonnay, rested on the floor beside two glasses.

Martin held his hand out. "Are you coming in?"

"Wow!" She managed, before a tear slipped down her cheek.

Martin sighed and took her back in his arms. "You, my sweetheart, are overtired. When did you last eat?"

Christie mumbled something against his chest. His scent filled her with longing to stay exactly where she was, but her growling stomach was just as insistent she move.

"I hope you just said you had lunch today. And breakfast?"

"I just wanted to finish and get home."

"We'll discuss this another time. Wine?"

Randall flopped down in the doorway. His tail thumped on the ground when Christie patted his soft head. "Missed you."

She was home. Everything was right here.

"Who needs a dining room table?" Christie sat cross-legged on the floor, wine glass in one hand and a piece of bread in the other.

"Might get uncomfortable after a while."

"I might buy big cushions. Or bean bags."

"I hope not."

With a grin, Christie toasted him. "To you, with thanks."

"You're welcome. For what?"

"This. Painting my bedroom and making my bed. Being here when I got home."

Martin leaned over to kiss her forehead. "I should have told you we were here."

"You were right. I was overtired and hungry. Silly of me to react like that!" Her face tensed up.

"Here. Come here." He held his arm out and Christie shuffled over a bit to move into his embrace. With his free hand, he refilled their glasses.

"How was Melbourne?"

"Exhausting. Don't get me wrong, I love the job still and I adore Docklands Studios. It was just… weird. Being back there."

"Did you see him?"

Christie's eyes flew to Martin's. Worry creased his brow.

"No! Of course not. I promised I'd stay clear and I did."

"But Docklands is small. That was my concern, that he'd run into you somehow."

"Ash and Ray took me out for dinner at Central Pier which is straight past my old apartment. But they had already seen him go out in a taxi and were with me every moment. So protective and sweet. And they walked me almost back to the hotel. Well, we ran a bit, 'cos it was raining."

Martin chuckled.

Eyes closed in contentment, Christie relaxed against Martin. How silly she was, imagining Derek would even bother with her anymore. That part of her life was over and now she had the most wonderful future to look forward to.

had been no warmth about Gran. Bringing her orphaned grandchild into her sterile home was a huge imposition and Dorothy had made sure Christie knew it.

Christie touched Gran's headstone. At least now, she was at rest. Such a pity she would never know Martha was reunited with Thomas. If nothing else, Gran's insistence on Christie delving into the past had brought her to Martin.

By late afternoon the cottage was quiet again. Christie swept debris into a pile. The other bedroom and the dining room had new ceilings, primed walls and bare floorboards. Old carpet slumped in a pile near the front gate, waiting for the over-full bin on the verge to be emptied.

The familiar sound of a motorcycle interrupted the silence. Christie smoothed her hair and hurried out.

Helmet dangling from one hand, Martin stood beside the motor-cycle, surveying the garden. His customary t-shirt clung to a muscular chest and flat stomach, and he wore jeans. Denim that hugged the contours of his legs right up to his narrow waist, curving over his…

Stop it!

Christie's heart skipped a beat as he turned a leisurely smile on her.

"You've been busy."

"It's a bit of a mess. But at least the roses are back under control."

"So I see." He dropped the helmet on the seat and closed the gap between them. He checked her hands, criss-crossed with small cuts and grazes. "You've put something on these?"

"They're just from the thorns."

"And?"

"I washed my arms. I need to get a first aid kit, or something."

"How long since a tetanus shot?"

"Last year."

Stop fussing.

Christie gently extricated her arm. "What's the helmet for?"

"Safety. Yours."

Her eyes lit up. "Oh, where are we going?"

"Somewhere I don't think you've been yet. So, get yourself ready and lock up."

"Do you want to come in?" She grinned.

"No. I want you to hurry up!"

Still smiling, she rushed inside.

The last time Christie was on this motorcycle, the Lotus had run out of fuel and Martin reluctantly helped her get some. Then he had whisked her up the nearby mountain to a lookout, where he had accused her of planning to bring development into the town.

This time they rode past Palmerston House, the stately homestead once owned by Christie's family for generations and now run as a bed and breakfast. Martin slowed as a new housing estate came into view along the right at the top of the hill. The few finished homes were large, on bigger than normal blocks, but still like suburbia. One road led into the estate, through stone walls proclaiming "River's End Heights".

The road curved inland. It was bushy, the sea disappearing from sight. With hardly a touch of the brakes, Martin swung left onto a narrow track, Christie gripping his waist. She gazed ahead as the trees parted. Here was a secluded bay, much smaller than the beach at River's End. Protected by cliffs almost wrapping around the narrow strip of sand, the calm water looked deep. And it was dotted with yachts.

Fingers entwined, Martin and Christie followed a path to the shore. The motorcycle was in a parking bay, one of ten or so marked out at the end of the track.

"How long has this been here?" Eyes wide with excitement, Christie almost skipped along.

"It's a natural harbour, so probably centuries, but the new estate we passed increased the population of boats."

"I thought there were more around. Oh, look at that one!" She pointed to a schooner.

"Yes. Pick the most expensive one."

"You used to accuse me of collecting expensive toys. Never considered a boat though."

"But you'd like one?" Martin glanced sideways.

"My own yacht? That's beyond my pay cheque."

"If it wasn't?"

Christie stopped as they neared the edge of the sand, surveying the bay. Ten or twelve craft of different sizes and types bobbed at their moorings. Her eyes were drawn to a smaller yacht, sleek and older in style. How wonderful to sail it out between the cliffs to the open sea.

"I would love it."

Martin pulled her close, tilting her chin up and touching his lips to hers. "And I love you." He turned her to face the boats. One arm around her waist, he pointed with the other. To the smaller yacht.

"Made from Huon pine in Tasmania. A sloop so responsive to sail that she can almost do it on her own."

"She is beautiful."

"She's old. But yes, she is beautiful."

The peace of early evening enveloped them. Surreal late sunlight flooded through the gap between the cliffs.

"Read the name."

The yacht was a fair way out, but Christie had good eyesight. As though highlighted by the sun, the name on the side of the boat was clear.

She shot a shocked glance at Martin.

"Read it, sweetheart."

"Her... her name is *Jasmine Sea*."

A BOAT OF FREEDOM

"But... how? Why?" Christie gripped Martin's hand to stop hers shaking.

"Take a deep breath."

"I don't need a breath! Why is the yacht called *Jasmine Sea*? Please?"

"Come and see." Martin released her hand and strode down the beach a short way. Christie caught up with him as he dragged a dinghy from a pile. The dinghy was small and timber and, to Christie's eye, unsafe. That didn't stop Martin pulling it all the way to the tideline. He fiddled with the oars.

"Are we getting in that?"

"Depends if you want to see the yacht. Or you could swim."

"It might be safer."

"Have I ever put you in danger?"

She grabbed one side of the dinghy. "What are we waiting for?"

Martin's eyes missed nothing. "Toss your shoes in. Once we're knee deep, hop in and I'll get us a bit further out."

Shoes and socks went in and she took a moment to roll her jeans up to her knees. His idea of knee deep water was different than hers, and it wasn't long before her legs were wet.

"Okay, sit in first and then take your legs over. That's the way."

Martin steered the small boat a bit further out, then copied Christie's actions to join her. He rowed effortlessly through the small waves. "I thought you knew how to sail?"

"A fifty-footer. A big boat and it was tied up in a marina, so no need to row to it."

As he navigated round a larger yacht, Martin gestured at the water. "It isn't very deep here. No more than we swim in. Check out how clear it is."

He was right. The sandy bottom seemed close enough to touch. The sea was calm and she turned her attention to the yacht now only a moment away.

Jasmine Sea was a picture as she gently rocked. Her long bow was graceful, with shining ankle-high railings, and tall timber masts towering above the cabin and wheel.

At the stern, a ladder invited Christie to climb on board Padded seats and a fold out table made a perfect place to enjoy a meal. Near the cabin was a timber wheel. Steps led below deck.

Christie turned to Martin. She needed to know. Unfazed, he leaned against the railing, arms crossed.

"This is yours?"

"No. Actually, yes. For now."

"I don't follow."

"I've owned this craft for years. One of the first things I ever bought. Over time, I've used her less and less. Although Randall still loves being on board."

"You have a boat called *Jasmine Sea?*"

A tiny flicker of impatience crossed his face. "I had a boat called – well, called something else. Whilst you were in Melbourne, I changed her name. And now she is *Jasmine Sea*. And if you want her, she is yours."

"Oh."

"Oh?"

Why?

Who gives away their boat? They weren't married or engaged or... Her legs shook. Was he about to propose?

"Whoa, steady. Here, sit for a while." Martin led her to the seats and took her onto his lap. He brushed stray hair from her eyes. "Slow breaths. Don't faint on me."

"Sorry. I just felt a bit odd for a moment. I'm okay now."

"Missing meals again?"

"Did you really say this is mine? Are you giving me a whole yacht?"

"Bit pointless giving you part of one. Maybe I should have waited."

She shook her head, struggling to understand. He sighed, wrapping both arms around her so that she leaned against his chest, her head on his shoulder.

"I've never had anyone to give things to. Christie, you've changed everything by being here. Being with me. But I see in your eyes sometimes that you're not sure."

She tried to sit up but he tightened his hold a little, adjusting his position so that she could see his face.

"I love you, Martin!"

"Sometimes love isn't enough. You have another world out there and I know you're torn."

"What are you saying?"

Martin kissed the tip of her nose. "I'm saying this boat is your freedom. Use it anytime you want to escape. For an hour or a week. This is its harbour, just as I am yours."

"I love my job. And I miss my apartment sometimes. And my friends. But this is my world now, at least for the most part. With you." Her voice was barely above a whisper.

"And Randall."

"Yes, actually, where is Randall?"

"Having a sleepover at Palmerston."

Christie giggled. "May I explore my boat?"

"Soon." His lips touched hers. "Once I've done this for a while."

The bedroom at the bow was simple and comfortable with a freshly made bed. There was a tiny bathroom and a functional galley with a

"What is it called?"

"Coffee. And this is bacon, which comes from..."

"Very funny. This place?"

"Willow Bay. Named for the native willows along the ridge. This has been her home for longer than I've lived."

"I never knew it was here. So hidden and perfect."

"Not completely perfect – there are a few spots to be careful of. The channel is pretty safe, but there are a couple of tricks to avoid trouble."

"But you'll teach me?"

"Every step of the way."

In the dinghy, heading back to shore, Christie was silent. She watched Martin row, powerful sweeps of the oars cutting through the water with next to no effort. How could he be so good at everything?

"What's wrong?"

"Nothing. Okay. Actually, turns out I can't sail after all."

Martin put the oars down and let the dinghy drift. He took both of Christie's hands in his, rubbing their palms. "Actually, you can. It takes time to understand each boat, and this one is old. She has some idiosyncrasies."

"But how could I ever handle *Jasmine Sea* on my own? She's so responsive in your hands but I made her stop."

"Practice. Doing the marine course will help, and so will I." He kissed each hand then picked up the oars.

"Can we sail somewhere? For a few days?"

"When you get that cottage of yours finished, then yes. We'll take Randall and go down the coast a bit."

"So he really likes the boat?"

"Loves it."

The dinghy bumped through the waves near the beach and Martin clambered out. Christie joined him, helping pull the little boat to shore. She lost her grip and sat down in the shallow water.

Martin held out a hand, laughing. He pulled her to her feet, keeping her hand in his and dragging the dinghy along. "I think you need a life jacket."

"That's not funny." She spluttered, trying to wipe wet hair from her eyes. "I look a mess now!"

"Yes. But in a beautiful mermaid kind of way."

She stopped, slipping her hand from his. He kept going, getting the dinghy high up the beach and turning it upside-down. Then, he wandered back to the shore, grinning.

"Are you going to stand in the waves all day, or would you like to go home?"

"I'm a mermaid. I can't leave the sea."

In response, Martin strode into the water and swept Christie into his arms, lifting her as though she weighed nothing. "Always wanted a mermaid and now I have one." He stood, legs apart to brace himself. "So, which is it? Go home and have a shower, or..."

"Or what?"

"Or I throw you back in." He turned as if to follow through.

Christie wrapped her arms tightly around his neck. "Home! I mean, I'd like to go home."

"But mermaids live in the sea. And besides, you forgot something."

Giggling, Christie nestled into his arms. "Please. Take me home, please?"

"Much better. Manners are important for mermaids." A car door slammed at the parking area. "And that is our cue to leave." Martin murmured, stepping onto the beach and gently placing Christie back on her feet.

A hot shower had rarely felt so good. The ride home on the motorcycle resulted in semi-dry, cold clothes that she was relieved to peel off. Martin had dropped her at the end of the driveway and Christie had watched him go, part of her longing to leave with him. It had always been this way, even early on when they were at odds with each other. The minute they were apart, she missed him.

With a sigh, Christie turned off the shower and reached for a towel. Her relationship with Derek had never felt like this. When they dated, she enjoyed being with him, but was just as happy to go back to her apartment and plan her next job, or go out with friends. Even once he moved in with her, there had not been this longing to be together all the time.

Christie stopped drying her hair and stared in the mirror.

Jasmine Sea.

Words that had significantly mattered at pivotal moments in her relationship with Martin. Now, he had changed the name of his own yacht.

You don't deserve it.

More than once in the past, Martin had mentioned what he called her expensive toys. Her car, Derek's very expensive ring. Even a new phone when she threw hers against a wall to stop it ringing.

Now he had given her the most expensive toy of all, for she had no doubt the yacht was worth more than the cottage Gran left behind. It felt wrong.

Perhaps it was not the gift itself she didn't deserve. Perhaps it was his love.

SURPRISE AND DISAPPOINTMENT

Palmerston House was as impressive in its modern role as a bed and breakfast, as when it was the stately home of the Ryan family. Immaculate gardens enticed weary travellers to wander and enjoy the European-inspired beauty. Wide verandahs offered views of the gardens from seating nooks. The sprawling pond out the back was busy with birdlife.

"Oh, I thought I heard your car!" Elizabeth White hurried down the curved stairway from the mezzanine level.

"Yes, I have no hope of sneaking anywhere quietly!" Christie met her at the bottom of the steps and kissed her cheek. "You look well."

"Not having to worry about those newlyweds helps!"

"Have you heard from Martha?"

"Only a one-minute phone call when they arrived in Dublin. Shall we have tea?" Elizabeth didn't wait for a response.

Christie followed her down the picture-studded hallway. There were framed photographs of old timber yards, the industry that elevated the Ryan family's fortunes. The railway station in its heyday, bustling with people and activity. Members of the Ryan family across many decades. At the very end was an empty hook. Faint differences

"I'd offer you dinner, but there's a potential client who's arranged to call me soon. I'll be a while."

"Oh. I'll go? That's what you mean. Oh, I thought..."

"What did you think?"

"No, nothing."

"I'm sorry, I'd have liked to spend the evening together. Tomorrow?" He kissed her. She barely returned the pressure of his lips and he pulled away to look at her. "I've upset you."

Christie pushed down the feelings of bitter disappointment and embarrassment. She smiled and handed him her empty glass. "Actually, I'm rather tired so yes, let's catch up tomorrow."

Martin searched her face, his forehead creased. "We'll talk about this then."

"Sure."

Not a chance.

"I hope the phone call goes well." She ran down the steps.

"Christie?"

"Give Randall a cuddle!" Without a backward glance, she hurried into the evening, hoping he wouldn't follow.

11

LOVE AND OTHER
MISUNDERSTANDINGS

I n near-darkness, Christie stood at Dorothy's grave. What on earth was wrong with herself? Gran had thrown away marriage after marriage. Pushed away everyone who loved her. Lived a lonely life for decades.

I don't want that!

Hands clenched, Christie stalked away. What if she was making the same mistake with Martin that she'd made with Derek? So desperate to be loved, she'd allowed Derek to move in with her only weeks after meeting him. And her life was good. Fulfilled, busy, successful. But not happy.

At the side of the road she waited for a car to pass. The driver tooted and Daphne Jones waved madly as she and John passed. The tension drained away the moment Christie waved back at the couple who'd been the first to welcome her to town all those months ago. This wasn't her old life. This was her hang-up, not Martin's. He had no idea of her state of mind. Imagining a proposal not once but twice in a couple of days was silly.

The old railway station loomed on the right through the trees lining her street. Once the hub for transport and freight for the region, the old buildings were long deserted and falling apart.

Nobody ever stepped onto the platform to wait for a loved one to return.

Clank.

The sound reverberated from somewhere along the line, startling Christie. She opened the flashlight app on her phone.

There was the crack of a branch, or maybe just the wind in the trees, closer now.

"Hello? Who's there?" Christie's eyes shot from one side of the road to the other, following the light from her phone. There was no answer. She hurried to the driveway.

At the gate she paused, glancing back. It must have been an animal, perhaps a possum or kangaroo. Her imagination was on overdrive. Unfamiliar fear crept into her mind and she rushed past the Lotus to the back door.

The cottage was a mess. Scattered throughout the hallway, kitchen, and lounge room were leftover pieces of plaster and debris. The dining room and lounge room – now the main focus of the renovation – housed piles of paint-splattered drop sheets, ladders, and an assortment of plasterboards.

Christie leaned against the doorway to the lounge room. She'd got the workmen to throw the old sofa into the rubbish bin out the front. After stepping over the drop sheets, she ran a hand over the marble mantelpiece. It needed to come off so Barry's men could repair large cracks in the wall behind it. Not long ago, a seascape had hung above the fireplace, repaired and framed by Martin. Now it belonged to Thomas and Martha, back with its artist and the woman he painted it for.

Hungry, she navigated around the mess to the kitchen. Behind a bottle of wine she found some leftover chili con carne. As it heated, she made good use of the short wait to open the wine. The moment she sat at the table, Martin's ringtone filled the room.

"Do you mind doing the talking?" she said.

"Why?"

"Eating." Without waiting for an answer, she took a mouthful. "Mmm."

He chuckled. "Very good. Sorry about earlier, just never know how long these things take."

"S'okay."

"S'okay? No, don't answer. You're not making any sense." He paused, sipping on something. Probably whiskey. "When I finished the call about the new commission, I got one from Thomas."

Almost choking in an attempt to swallow, Christie grabbed her wine and forced the food down. "Are they o-okay?" She coughed a bit at the end.

"I thought you wanted me to do the talking? They are fine. Loving it in fact. Thomas wants you to know that Martha's little house is a lot like your cottage, except it has a front door."

"You didn't ask him about my front door? Oh my goodness! If he wants a front door, then there will be one when they get back and that way they can have the cottage. Oh, I'm so happy!"

"Are you quite finished?" He was amused. "No, I didn't. We got onto other things."

"What other things? When are they coming home?"

"Eat and I'll tell you. Are you eating?"

Christie filled her mouth again.

"Martha has put her place up for sale. There's already been a few interested people and she's finding it a bit… confronting. Thomas is whisking Martha off to Paris. Apparently, they had some plan to go there once. He is so excited, sounds like a young man."

I will meet you anytime, anywhere you want me to. We can move to Paris if you wish. Get far away from River's End and start a new life for ourselves. Just do not give up on us.

That was what Thomas once wrote to Martha, in a letter she never saw. There'd been other mentions of Paris, but that one came back to Christie with alarming clarity.

"You don't think they are staying there?"

"What do you mean?"

"Permanently. Like, moving to Paris."

"No. Relax, sweetheart, it is just a long overdue visit."

"You know he once told her they could move there. Leave here forever. What if that's what they're doing?" Near tears, Christie pushed her plate away.

Martin took a moment to reply. "It isn't. They're not going to leave you. Nor am I."

"Then why don't you…" She stopped herself.

"Why don't I what? Christie, what am I not doing?"

"Let's talk about something else. Okay?"

Please, let it go.

A long silence drew out between them. Appetite gone, Christie played with her wine glass.

Eventually, with a sigh, Martin spoke. "How was the walk home? Did you go via the beach?"

"Yes. It got dark quickly and I put the flashlight on when I thought…"

"Thought what?"

Christie stared at the ceiling. "There was a possum or something up along the railway track." She forced a laugh. "It made me jump, that's all."

"Maybe I should come over."

"No. I mean, it isn't necessary. I'm safely here and the door is locked. And look, I'm even eating. I just want to clean up the mess the tradies left today and have an early night. But, thanks."

"I could tuck you into bed."

"Stop tempting me. I love you."

"I love you as well. A lot."

After he hung up, Christie held the phone for a while. More than anything she wanted him here but how could she be honest without the emotion? Swirling around in her head were too many what ifs and doubts. Not just about their future, but Thomas and Martha's.

Martin whistled for Randall as he strode across the soft grass to the gate. Running to catch up with him, the dog – tail wagging furiously – was ready for the night-time adventure. Hand on the gate, Martin stopped.

Would turning up uninvited on Christie's doorstep make things worse? He'd seen her hide some sudden emotion before she'd left. Just now, her tone of voice and odd comments reinforced his gut feeling that something was upsetting her.

Earlier, on the deck, their connection had been strong. Her hands on his chest, her eyes gazing at him with such incredible love. With the late rays of the sun on her face, no woman in the world was more beautiful. So fragile and precious, she created a desire in him almost impossible to keep in check.

If it was up to him, they would be married tomorrow. They would have a family, the dream he'd kept buried his whole life. Only now, with the light she brought, could he begin to imagine this was real.

Martin wandered back to the house, trailed by a confused Randall. He had to step back a little and give her some space. If he rushed her into a commitment, then he was no better than Derek.

At the deck, Martin dropped onto the top step. Randall whined and offered him a paw. "Sorry, mate. False alarm." He scratched the dog's head, staring into the night.

Once he had been in a happy family. His mother singing him to sleep. Dad carrying him on his shoulders. Vague memories that disappeared a little more every year.

After a lifetime of loneliness, Christie burst into his world. He needed to protect and love her, inhale her scent, and walk in the light she radiated. Every time she was out of his sight, he ached to hear her laugh. See her smile.

The only way to do this was slowly. One step at a time, letting her lead, so she would know he was serious and not be afraid of embracing this precious love they shared.

12
_____

DOOR TO THE PAST

R ain on the window woke Christie before dawn. She snuggled
under the covers. Sleep was elusive, pushed aside by annoying
memories of Derek. He'd been so attentive at the beginning and she'd
missed all the warning signs of his narcissism. Over time, as her
friends drifted away and few took their place, he became her world,
outside of work.

No doubt she'd compensated by concentrating on her career.
Perseverance paid off, fulfilling her until the day he and Ingrid ripped
it away. How naive she'd been. Well, those two suited each other and,
hopefully, would never appear in her life again.

On the other hand, Martin was a real alpha male, naturally protective and, at times, bossy. Yet this felt right. More than right. Christie
was an intelligent, educated and sensible woman, able to stand up for
herself and others. Yet all Martin needed to do was raise an eyebrow
or lower his voice to that mild yet no-nonsense tone and she was not
only listening, she was melting.

She gave up on sleep and turned on the bedside lamp. Christie
picked up the photo Belinda had given her. A moment in time she
would always treasure. This was the man she loved and if he needed

time to decide she was his future wife, then so be it. After all, she had a cottage to finish before Martha and Thomas returned.

———

Breakfast was coffee and a reminder in her phone to go shopping. By the time Barry and his men arrived, the rain was gone, leaving a grey but warm enough morning. Two of the men started pulling the mantelpiece apart, whilst Barry and another man turned their attention to the closet at the end of the hallway.

Christie stayed in the kitchen, making a shopping list as she listened to them work. In a few days the bathroom, laundry, and kitchen would be gutted and, at that point, she would move out. Elizabeth insisted she go to Palmerston House and, unless Martin suggested otherwise, Christie would do that.

"Christie?" Barry called from the hallway.

Almost at a sprint, Christie joined him.

He grinned at her. "So, would you like a front door?"

"It's doable?"

"Sure is. From the look of things, this here," he tapped on the closet "was the doorway. Where the weatherboard is outside would have been a little entry alcove. We'll start from this side, restructure as needed, put a door in. The outside can wait until the cottage is secure."

"I want the cottage to be like it once was."

"Okay then. I'll give you links to a couple of door places and if you can take a peek and give me some options, we'll order one." Barry tapped on his iPad and a moment later Christie's phone beeped.

Back at the table, she compared the old door in the photograph to those on the sites Barry had sent. The original door was solid timber, nothing inviting or interesting.

Forget tradition.

Christie sent a message back to Barry with a link to a timber door with glass inserts featuring kookaburras,

A moment later he stuck his head around the door. "Good choice.

It'll come up a treat with some stain. I'll also order a lightweight security screen door."

"Oh, okay. I guess it would be nice to have the front door open in summer."

"Best to have it anyway, what with the glass panels and all." He disappeared again.

Frowning, Christie wondered if she'd made the right choice. If someone wanted to break in, there were plenty of windows. Not that anyone would. It wasn't as if she had anything worth stealing.

The jewellery store door jangled as Christie pushed it open with her hip, hands full with two cups of takeaway coffee from the corner cafe.

George Campbell looked up from polishing a watch, a broad smile lighting his face. "What brings you by, my dear young lady?"

"Hello, George. Thought you might enjoy a coffee." Christie offered him one. "Just the way you like it."

"How thoughtful, thank you."

"Not entirely. It is kind of a swap for information, if you have a few moments?"

"For you, always." George reached for his coffee.

"You know I am renovating the cottage? Well, it has come to light that once upon a time, it had a front door. In fact, there is a photo belonging to Palmerston House showing one right in the middle of the front wall."

"Indeed. You certainly like to look into the past."

"Actually, I thought that was over, but I am curious about why anyone would change such a lovely building that way. Barry Parks says it may have been done anywhere from fifty to seventy years ago, going by the timber."

"Let me see. I am seventy-four, so it must have been about nineteen-sixty. Yes, it was, for I had turned seventeen and Tom was just sixteen. You need to understand his parents were very traditional. No encouragement for him to pursue art for goodness sake. His father,

James, wanted him to be the next stationmaster and they argued about it just before the two of us went on a weekend hike into the mountains. It is a sad story though."

George paused, brow furrowed.

"What happened?" Christie prompted.

"When we returned, I went up to the cottage with Tom to put the camping gear in the garage. It was late, and dark. Tom stopped in the middle of the driveway, not sure what was wrong, but then we realised the front door was gone. We joked about it. His parents were not very social people."

It must run in the family. Cliff top houses and mountain retreats.

"After stowing the gear away, I headed home so I only have his version of events." George sighed. "You really should speak to him about it, but he probably won't tell you anyway. All I know is that his father closed in the entry way. Tom had hung some of his paintings there, against his father's wishes. At the same time, his father threw away all of the paintings – his sketches, paints, brushes, everything."

"No! Oh, how horrible. How could a father do that to his own son?"

"Tom left home the same night and came to my house for a while. He was still at school and worked weekends at the timber yards. After a bit, his father apologised and Thomas went back. But it was never the same."

"There's a paint-splattered work bench in the attic."

"They reached a compromise. Thomas agreed to follow his father's footsteps in return for a workspace that was his alone."

"But he was never a stationmaster."

"The line closed. Happiest I'd seen Tom in years when it happened. By then, he had Martha and was working on selling some paintings before they married. So, there it is."

Christie squeezed George's arm. "I'm so sorry to remind you."

"The past is never far away these days. At least now, Thomas is happy, truly happy, and that, my dear, is your doing." He patted her hand.

13

TAKING WHAT'S OURS

Ingrid stalked into Derek's office with a scowl. He glanced up from his laptop, raised an eyebrow and looked back at the screen.

"Where is it?" She put both hands on the other side of the desk, leaning toward him. "And why?"

"Why what? I'm busy."

"The monstrosity of a painting. I might not like it, but I should be consulted before you just sell something off like that!"

The phone rang. Derek hit the intercom. "Hold my calls, Lorraine." He closed the laptop, pushed his chair back and crossed one ankle over his knee. "Careful. This is still my firm."

Ingrid inhaled slowly and straightened. "Sorry. Don't mean to be bossy but you know I'm used to running things." She swayed her hips as she stepped around the desk and deliberately sat on its edge as close to Derek as possible. "Don't be cross."

"Seeing as you're here, update me with your progress."

"Not much to tell. Had a lovely long conversation with lover-boy and he agreed to meet. Kept telling me he doesn't do portraits but I persuaded him I really need one. For my elderly mother, you know."

Of course. "What else?"

"While I am in town, there's a real estate agent, John Jones, who handles things for Bryce Montgomery's developments locally. Perhaps he needs a chance to consider… alternative options."

"Tread very softly and make sure you meet him away from his office. Not when that meddling wife of his is around." He had no doubt Daphne Jones had been responsible for alerting Martin Blake when he visited Chris last year. The memory of being thrown out of her cottage by Martin still angered him. "My name cannot come into it, if you insist on speaking to him."

Ingrid moved her legs so that they touched Derek's. "Did you upset things so badly?"

He returned the pressure. "Let's just say that they are fans of Chris. And that artist. Tread gently."

"I heard you the first time. Where is the painting?"

"You do your job and I," he got to his feet and walked to a small bar. "I will take care of mine."

After pouring two glasses of brandy, Derek wandered back to the desk and handed one to Ingrid. "To taking what's ours." Their glasses clinked.

"To loads of money." Ingrid replied.

14

A SOLE SURVIVOR

O nce Christie unpacked the shopping, she followed the echo of hammering down the hallway. As usual, debris and dust covered the floor and it got worse by the minute. Barry stood aside as one of his men pounded on newly exposed brickwork between the bedrooms.

"Sorry." Barry raised his voice over the noise. "Whoever did this went to a lot of effort to make it solid. Two rows of bricks."

"It was the stationmaster."

"Huh? Hey, Dave, take a break."

Happy to put his tools down, the other man nodded to Christie and headed toward the kitchen.

"I said it was the stationmaster himself that did this. The last one."

Barry rubbed his forehead. "Was he hiding a body?"

"Where's the cupboard?"

"Garage. Boys got it out in one piece so it'll make good storage out there if you want. Which reminds me, you had a delivery."

"Me? But I haven't ordered anything."

"Are you sure? It's pretty big. We signed for it, hope that's okay, and put it in the garage as well. Here, I'll show you."

Christie followed Barry, glancing into the lounge room as they passed. The walls were ready for painting and the mantelpiece back in place. She couldn't wait to decorate the room.

Inside the garage, a large, thin box – much like one housing a giant flat screen television – leaned against a wall. Something about its size and shape was familiar. Christie glanced at Barry. "Do you know who sent it?"

"Just a regular delivery van. Barely fitted in."

Christie looked for a return address.

"Want me to open it?" Barry pulled out a box knife and when Christie nodded, sliced carefully along one seal. He peered inside. "Art."

Sudden dread filled Christie. With uncanny insight, she knew what it was. As Barry sliced through the other sides, she opened her mouth to stop him, but nothing came out. He pulled the front away, then thinner packing board behind it.

"Wow! This is one fine painting." Barry stood back to admire it, missing the fear that swept into Christie's face.

It was a fine painting. One that she loved as much as she loved its artist. The problem was that *Sole Survivor* belonged to Derek.

"Why? Just why?"

Christie paced around the garage. Martin stood like a rock some way back from the painting in silent thought.

"What on earth is Derek up to? This has to be some sort of screwed up message from him but why?" As Christie stomped past Martin for the third time, he reached out and gathered her into his arms. In the safety of his embrace, her heartbeat gradually slowed. Fear and frustration seeped away until Martin's steady breathing surrounded her.

"I don't know. But you being distressed doesn't help us work it out." Martin kissed Christie's forehead before releasing her.

"Sorry. It just shocked me."

"I can see that. You're sure there was no note?"

"Barry helped me search. Unless something fell off inside the delivery van, then no. And I've checked all the packing and box."

"An anonymous gift."

"Are you sure he bought it? I know he said he did, but that might have been to rattle me because I'd defended you when we first saw it." Christie gazed at the painting, absorbing the stunning colours.

"I am sure. The receipt was from his business. What do you mean you defended me?"

"He and Ingrid made some stupid comments about abstract art and I disagreed."

"And?"

"And... I may have been rather forceful and offended them. But it was their own fault! Ingrid declared abstract art is the work of a disorganised mind and I pointed out that you have one of the most logical, intelligent minds I know. Or something along those lines. Why are you smiling?"

"Because I adore you, my little ball of fire."

"Well, I wasn't about to stand there and let that woman judge you with no basis for her ridiculous comments."

"It really doesn't matter what other people think. You know that. Only the people you love matter."

Christie touched the man in the painting. Misshapen, he dragged an anchor twice his size from a broken shipwreck. All the colours were back to front and haunting.

Sole Survivor.

The person left behind when all around him was lost. She turned to Martin, emotion choking her voice. "This is you."

He didn't answer, just bit his bottom lip. She didn't need him to say a word. His eyes gave away more than he probably intended.

15

WANTING TOO MUCH

M artin locked the garage and handed Christie the key. "We need to decide what to do with it. I'm not comfortable with it staying here."

"In the garage? I guess it isn't the best place."

"No, here at the cottage. You have enough to worry about without this as well."

"Oh, that reminds me. Come and see what's going on!" Smiling at last, Christie took Martin's hand and they wandered to the cottage. "You won't believe what we're doing!"

"Installing a proper kitchen with appliances that order and prepare your meals?" Martin teased. "Gutting the cottage to open a cinema showing all the films you've worked on? Ouch, don't dig your nails into my hand. Let's see, turning a room into a beauty salon?"

Christie stopped at the back door to pat Randall, who lay fast asleep in the late afternoon sun. He groaned and rolled over to have his chest scratched and Christie obliged. "That's not a bad idea."

"Which one?" Martin leaned against a post to watch them interact.

"I could open a salon. Probably not here though, just a bit too far from town." She tilted her head. "You know, I don't believe anyone provides beauty services, apart from hairdressing." She gazed at Martin.

"Don't ask me. I was joking."

"Of course."

"It would interfere with your career."

"Yes. It would."

"Not give you the income you're used to."

"Are you trying to talk me out of it?" Christie took his hand again, playing with his fingers, keeping her eyes on his. "I'd be in River's End all the time. No more travelling. No more absences." Which was what Derek used to complain about. "I love living here." She opened the door.

Martin caught up with her in the lounge room. He inspected the wall above the mantelpiece. "Nice job. Once the room's painted, I'll find you a painting."

"It suits the seascape. Thomas' painting. So I do hope they'll accept the cottage as a gift."

"There's a lot of history here. It is incredibly sweet that you want this so much, but what if they can't get past that history?"

"I don't know. I shall probably sell. But, hopefully it won't come to that. Particularly once Thomas sees what we're doing with the front door."

"You found out about it."

"I went to see George and he told me when and why it was closed off. Poor Thomas, he was only sixteen... oh, you don't know." Christie turned away and went to the window. The trees cast long shadows with the approach of evening. After a moment, Martin came to stand behind her, his hands resting on the windowsill, one on either side of Christie.

"What I do or don't know is beside the point. George should know better than to discuss Thomas behind his back."

"He was trying to help. Not being a gossip and after all he was there when it happened."

"It isn't your business though. Nor mine. Stop trying to fix everything, sweetheart."

Christie's heart sank as she stared at their reflections in the window, Martin's face so hard, like it had been time and again when they first met.

Why don't you trust me?

"I'm sorry. I won't speak of it again, but I will put the front door back where it belongs. As you said, Martha and Thomas may not wish to live here, so I need to think about myself, or the value of the place should I sell."

"Who would you sell it to? It seems to be developers who want it."

"And you know I will never sell to them! I don't know who and anyway, it isn't my priority." She fell silent, aware that her voice had sharpened.

Martin moved his hands from the windowsill to Christie's waist, gently turning her to face him. She kept her eyes down.

"Christie? I'm not cross with you."

Still, she stared at their shoes. He chuckled and in surprise, her eyes flew to his.

"You want to say something. And you're holding it in."

She tightened her lips into a straight line and stepped out of his loose embrace. "Would you like to stay for dinner?"

"Yes, but don't get defensive and change the subject. Tell me what you're thinking."

I'm scared of loving you too much. I want a family with you but what if I lose everything? What if you don't feel the same?

"I'd rather not, just now. I might go and see what looks good to cook though." She softened her tone and managed a small smile.

Martin nodded. "I need to feed Randall. We'll be back in a little while."

"I love you."

"I know you do." Martin squeezed her hand on his way past and left Christie alone in the lounge room.

Just after dark, Christie heard a familiar woof from the street. Such a little thing to make her happy, yet it did, so much. Randall was the dog she'd never had as a child. Gran would not tolerate any pets, not even a goldfish, leaving Christie to daydream about owning a cat, or a dog. Sometimes even a donkey, with long velvety ears.

She turned on the back light and unlocked the door, then returned to stirring a bolognaise sauce. Martin knocked.

"It's unlocked," she called.

"It shouldn't be." Carrying a bottle of wine and a small chiller bag, Martin came in with Randall. "Do we need to discuss this, Christie?"

His tone reminded her of the day he'd found the door unlocked after twice reminding her to lock it. A shiver went up her spine. Part apprehension and part attraction. She waved her spoon at him. "I only unlocked it when I heard Randall bark. I promise it was locked before then."

After leaving the wine and chiller bag on the kitchen table, Martin wandered to the stove. He kissed Christie's cheek. "Smells fantastic. Keep the door locked please. Particularly at night." He took wine glasses from a cupboard. "Perhaps you should get some lights around the cottage as well?"

"Why? This is a safe town, how often have I heard you say that? Everyone says it, in fact." As a pot of water came to the boil, Christie turned down the sauce and collected fresh pasta from the fridge. She added salt and oil to the water, then the pasta.

"Shall I stir?" Martin took a spoon to the pasta anyway and Christie stopped what she was doing to watch him with a grin. "What?"

"I just like looking at you."

Martin turned off the sauce and opened the wine, but with just a hint of a smile that filled Christie's heart.

"Randall's gone to your bedroom. Is that okay?" He handed Christie a glass of wine. "Cheers."

"Cheers. He can sleep wherever he wants."

"Yes, he has that effect on people all the time."

"Mmm."

"What does 'mmm' mean?"

Christie took a sip of wine before answering. "He is so special. I'd like to have a dog one day but how on earth would I get one like him?"

"He's one of a kind, like they all are. You know he has chosen you as one of his people? It isn't a case of who owns Randall, but who Randall wants to be with. You're definitely high on that list."

"But—"

"No buts." Martin busied himself finding cutlery. "Who am I to tell him who to love? It's not as though I don't feel the same."

Then why are you holding back so much?

Christie turned away so he wouldn't see the conflict in her eyes. Somehow, she had to learn patience.

16

DINNER FOR TWO

Dinner was long finished and the washing up underway. In between kisses, Martin washed and Christie dried. Randall sat hopefully in the middle of the kitchen. With no scraps coming his way, he wandered off again.

"The kitchen will be so wonderful once it's done." Christie folded the tea towel. "Coffee?"

"Thank you. You're putting a lot into it. If it really is all for Thomas and Martha, then they need to buy it."

Christie stopped filling the kettle to look at Martin in surprise. "I couldn't do that!"

"And why not? Martha is selling her home in Ireland and Thomas – assuming he agrees – will sell his little place up the mountain. On top of that, he's made a decent living as an artist for a long time, so money is not an object."

The kettle plugged in, Christie collected mugs and teaspoons, giggling as Martin barricaded the drawer by leaning against it and refusing to move until she kissed him. "You can make the coffee if you don't stop!"

"Perhaps I should. Do I need to buy you a coffee machine?"

"There's nothing wrong with yours."

"Except it's at my house."

"Exactly. So why we would need two?" Christie sneaked a glance at Martin. He was opening the chiller bag he'd brought with him. He mustn't have heard.

"What's in there?"

"Aunt Sylvia sent them."

"Sylvia? How sweet… and surprising," Christie joined Martin. "Did she know you were coming here?"

"Behave. She likes you a lot. Just give her time to get over Belinda moving to Melbourne."

"I like her too. It must be hard for her without Belinda, particularly in the bakery. Does she have anyone else to help? Ooh!" Her eyes got rounder as Martin lifted two perfect mini cheesecakes out of the bag and she rushed to the cupboard to find plates.

"To answer your question, yes, she has taken on a lad to train up. She had been considering an apprentice for a while, so in some ways this forced her to do it. He's a good kid, committed and keen."

Cheesecake on plates and coffee in hand, they settled back at the kitchen table. Christie smiled. "Between Belinda and now Sylvia, I have no chance of wasting away. I am pleased about her new assistant. She's done it tough, hasn't she?"

"Aunt Sylvia is a tough lady. And kind."

"Very. Was there ever a Mister Sylvia? Don't look at me that way, I'm not gossiping, just trying to fill in back story."

"It's her story to tell, but to stop you putting your foot in it, no there never was. Belinda and Jess' father would never commit to marriage and eventually, he moved on. No." He put his hand up as Christie went to ask more. "That's it. You want to know more, you ask Sylvia."

Christie gave him a little smile as collected the plates and went to the sink. "Another coffee?"

Martin checked his watch and stood up. "Time to let you get some sleep."

"I'm not tired."

"You should be, with all the work you're doing here." Martin held his arms out and Christie snuggled into his warmth. "I have an early meeting to prepare for."

"Banker? Insurance broker?" she teased.

"Are you free in the afternoon? Might go for a sail if you'd like to keep practising."

"That would be wonderful!"

Martin whistled softly and a moment later, Randall padded down the hallway, yawning. Christie followed them out onto the back porch.

"Sweet dreams. Lock the door."

"I will. Have a nice walk home."

Now wide awake, Randall took off after a rabbit. "My cue." Martin squeezed Christie's hand before following Randall into the darkness.

―――――――――

At almost midnight, Christie pushed her laptop away and made another coffee. In the last couple of hours she'd filled her head with nautical terms and rules of sailing, preparing for the Marine Licence exam. There were quite a few differences from what she'd learnt in California, sailing around Santa Monica with some of the cast of a film.

Those were heady days. In spite of her fear of the sea, and that she would embarrass herself being seasick, Christie had ended up on board the producer's yacht one evening and loved it.

There was a freedom in the wind-filled sails unlike any other. How cleanly and quietly the boat cut through the waves. More modern than *Jasmine Sea*, it comfortably carried the group out and around the gorgeous bay. One evening turned into many. Christie got on well with the producer, Carlo Palmero, and he gave everyone the chance to learn to sail.

It was extraordinary that she now had her own yacht. It didn't feel real and part of her still couldn't understand why. Did Martin believe that Christie needed the boat in order to feel at home?

Her phone announced a message with a soft beep and she almost squealed in delight. From Thomas, it was a photo taken in front of the Eiffel Tower. His arm was around Martha's shoulder and her eyes were on him. A message followed. *Highly recommend Paris for honeymoons.*

Christie responded with a smile. *Will keep that in mind. Lovely photo. Love you both!* How wonderful to see them in the place they'd once dreamed of going to. Their happiness was an inspiration. But were two happy endings in one family even possible?

17

PARIS

"What is that sound?" Thomas stopped in the middle of the park for the third time.

"I imagine it is your phone, dear." Martha took the opportunity to sink onto a bench. Thoughts of a foot rub had occupied her mind for the past hour, as Thomas directed them from one part of the beautiful city to another. His enthusiasm was admirable but her legs were suffering.

Phone in hand, Thomas joined Martha. "I think it's this thing here, then that... ah!" He held the phone back a bit to see. "From Christie. She wrote 'Will keep that in mind. Lovely photo. Love you both!'"

"That was quick! Isn't it midnight at home?"

"Maybe we woke her. Might need to work this out a bit better. What does she mean, 'will keep it in mind'? What could be better?"

"They're not even engaged, Thomas. Perhaps a little early to plan a honeymoon."

"Only took us a few weeks."

Martha leaned against Thomas and his arm went around her. "We had a lifetime to make up for."

"Not an hour passes that I forget that. Which is why we need to keep walking. There's so much to see."

"No, let's sit for a while. We can see perfectly well from here. I promised Christie I'd bring some photographs back."

As Martha opened her handbag, Thomas put his phone away. "This is the most incredible place. As you once promised it would be."

"What you could have accomplished had you come here as a young man! Paris would have been at your feet, my darling." Martha smiled at Thomas. "Tonight, I have something special arranged."

"Just how have you arranged anything? I thought I'd kept you close to me all the time."

"I have my ways. Did you know there is a restaurant below the glass pyramid in the Louvre?"

He shook his head.

"Well, there is. And, if you would care to escort me back to the hotel to have a short rest and get changed, then I will take you there."

"At night?"

"That's usually the best time for dinner, I find." She snapped a few photos of the park. "Unless you prefer not to visit the Louvre?"

"At night?"

"I'm certain you are repeating yourself. Yes, twice a week it is open late, so we can wander and gasp at the Mona Lisa and imagine ourselves part of a thriller book if we wish. But dinner is reserved for six-thirty, which is in about two hours—"

"Why are we sitting here?" Thomas was on his feet in an instant, hand held out for Martha. She took a moment to put the camera away, smiling to herself.

As soon as Martha stood up, Thomas wrapped his other around her body, pulling her close to him. "Do you have any idea how much I love you, Martha Blake?"

"Oh, yes I do. And I shall spend every day of my life the happiest woman in the world."

details.

Determined to make Melbourne his home, Angus had learnt to ignore his employer's sharpness and somehow won her over with his steady, calm, and perpetually polite nature. She retired around the time that Christie, her only grandchild, was orphaned and came to live with them. He flew to outback Queensland to attend the funeral and bring the child back. Dorothy would not forgive her own daughter for marrying the doctor who took her so far away, not even long enough to see her only offspring laid to rest.

Now, he had finished his final duty of emptying and selling the Toorak mansion. The Range Rover was his to keep, a car he rather liked. With nothing to hold him to Melbourne, he relished his recent travels around Victoria, following whatever road took his fancy. But it was Christie who always stayed in the back of his mind. The child, now woman, was as close to a daughter as he would ever have.

Almost dancing from room to room, Christie showed Angus the changes already made, and filled him in on the plans for the rest of the cottage. They stopped between the bedrooms.

"So here was once the front door." Christie waved at the brick wall. "Can you believe it was filled in last century and in all these years, nobody reversed that? Thomas lived here with his first wife, Frannie. Surely, they would have put the door back? Although..."

"Although?"

"Perhaps it hurt too much. His parents did this after there was an argument about Thomas' future. He wanted to paint and they wanted him to be the next stationmaster. According to his best friend, Thomas came home after a weekend hiking and not only was the door gone, but all of his paintings and art supplies. Thrown out."

"How awful! That would be life changing for a young man."

"It was. He eventually agreed to do as they wished in return for his own space to paint." She gestured above to the attic. "That is where he painted the seascape, Angus. And where Frannie hid the letters he once wrote to Martha so something must have stopped him using it, or she would never have kept them there."

"A sad story indeed. But your last email told me how happy Thomas and Martha are now."

"Come and have some tea. They are in Paris! I'll show you the photo they sent last night."

"I might just wash up first, if you don't mind?"

"Of course, ignore my chatter. I shall put the kettle on."

When Angus joined her a few moments later, he dropped the satchel onto the kitchen table. "I found some photos and bits and pieces from your Gran's you may wish to keep."

"No love letters from unknown people?" Christie handed him a cup of tea.

"Thank you. Not that I am aware of."

"Please, sit. Have you had breakfast?" She joined him with her coffee, pushing the satchel to one side. She'd open it later, when she was alone.

"Indeed. Quite a pleasant breakfast at the motel in Warrnambool."

"Speaking of motels, we need to find you somewhere to stay. I would have you here in a heartbeat but as you've seen, the place is only just habitable for me. As it is, I'll be moving out in a couple of days to let the guys do all the wet areas."

"Then it's a good thing I planned ahead and booked a room."

"You did? Not in that motel I hope!"

"No. At Palmerston House."

"Wonderful! Elizabeth will look after you and that's probably where I'll be soon as well. Oh, this is going to be so great. I don't know where to begin!"

20

A DECISION

M artin straddled his surfboard, aimlessly paddling in a circle of sorts. His mind drifted over the morning with his new client, Bethany Fox. He couldn't pick her accent, a curious mix of private school Australian, English and something else. German or Dutch. Or South African. She said she worked in finance and, from the look of her clothes and car, it was lucrative.

Under normal circumstances he would have politely declined. He usually only painted those who mattered to him, but two things swayed him. There was her own soft plea. This painting was for her parents in England. Her mother was frail and unable to travel. A lover of art, she asked Bethany for a portrait with Australian scenery around her daughter. Whilst Martin wondered why a quality photo-graph would not have sufficed, he nevertheless understood Bethany's desire to make her mother happy.

More importantly, there was the commission. Money usually mattered little to Martin. As long as he had enough to pay his debts and feed his dog, not much else counted. Thomas had taught him to save, to invest wisely. There was sufficient tucked away to keep him going for a long time should his income dry up. But that was before Christie came along.

He had to stop thinking like a single man. Sooner or later, she'd give him an indication that she was ready to be with him forever. If he was to be the man who would be the father of her children and the husband she deserved, then he needed to start planning for their future.

A small wave carried the surfboard in. Randall bounced around, barking happily. Martin put the surfboard under an arm and trudged through the sand toward his house. Much as it pained him to take time away from Christie, and go against his odd gut feeling, he'd made a decision. He'd ask for a ridiculous sum for the portrait and, if she agreed, he would paint Bethany Fox.

21

PHASE ONE

Ingrid drove past Palmerston House heading to River's End Heights. This was the first of Bryce Montgomery's development estates in the area. She snorted as she turned in through the stone entry walls. It was typical of so many developers to alienate the locals by creating a new suburb. The small town needed a massive upgrade and development so clever it would feel organic, which was the best way to get the nod from councils.

It took only a few moments to finish her inspection. About a hundred houses. No shops. No amenities apart from a tiny park in the middle. With only a handful of the houses occupied, it would be a while until the impact of a sudden population increase would filter to the village. One hundred families needing school placements, medical facilities and more shopping. How did Bryce think this would work?

She scanned the street, noting the boat trailers outside several homes. No boats on them, so there must be marina or harbour nearby. Interesting. Boats meant money and she was all about that.

Derek's ring-tone interrupted her thoughts. "Phase one underway," she answered.

"So, he's agreed?"

"Do you doubt me?"

"When do you start?"

"Still to be decided. Anyway, I'm seeing this estate agent shortly, so have had a drive around Bryce Montgomery's pathetic attempt at developing."

"You're keeping a low profile? Avoiding Chris? That would ruin—"

"For goodness' sake, Derek. I wasn't born yesterday." She softened her tone. "I won't let you down, but you need to trust me. Everything is meticulously planned." She followed the street back to the main road.

"Fine. Just be careful, the town is very insular."

"Insular or not, it is large enough for me to avoid exposure, as long as this John Jones character keeps his mouth shut."

"Presumably money will take care of it."

"I'll call you after my meeting."

"Good luck."

Luck is for gamblers.

Ingrid drove down the long hill that forked to either Martin's house or the town. She glanced at Palmerston House. The Lotus was there. No sign of Christie Ryan, but she would need to be careful if the other woman was in town today.

***

After an impromptu morning tea at Palmerston House, Christie reluctantly drove home. Angus insisted she keep her plans, promising to have dinner with her that evening. Elizabeth made him welcome and he was most comfortable in his new surroundings.

An empty car was parked opposite the cottage and Christie hoped it wasn't more property developers. The last time it was Bryce Montgomery and he was brazen enough to try to buy the place from under her. The older model sedan was not his style though, and she gave it no more attention.

Half an hour later, concentrating on shaping the roses along the front fence, Christie jumped and dropped her shears when a man walked into the driveway.

"Hey, I'm sorry!" Not quite as tall as Christie, suit jacket barely covering his girth, the man leaned down to retrieve the shears and handed them back. "I should have sung out."

Christie took the shears. "I was miles away."

"Beautiful garden."

"Thanks. It will be, once I finish it."

"I'm Rupert. How are you?" He offered his hand to shake. "I took a wrong turn and ran out of gas! At my age, one would think I'd know better."

"I've done that myself. Do you need me to call someone?"

"Oh, not at all. I walked down to the petrol station and just put some fuel in it."

Christie eyed his suit. "Would you like a glass of water?"

Rupert shook his head, then smiled. "Actually, yes. As long as I'm not imposing. My wife will be upset I forgot to carry water on the trip."

"Come around and I'll get you one. Where are you heading?"

"On my way home now. Bit disappointing really. I went to Warrnambool for a job interview. I'm in sales. We want a sea change, Lucy and I, now that we've got a bubba on the way."

They stepped onto the deck and Christie hesitated.

"Miss, I'm happy to wait here. Don't want to traipse dirt over your floor."

Christie broke into laughter. "Sorry to laugh. I'm renovating and the mess those tradies leave is more than you would imagine. Come in, please."

Rupert followed her, leaving the door open behind himself. He gazed around. "Miss, if you don't mind me saying, this is true old world charm."

She offered a glass of water to Rupert. "Please, I'm Christie. The cottage is rather special, isn't it? I'm looking forward to getting it back to its original beauty." The smell of cigarette smoke clung to his clothes and she took a discreet step back.

"Was it a stationmaster's residence?" Rupert gulped his water.

Christie took his glass and refilled it. "Thanks. Had no idea how thirsty I was. Long day."

"You said it was disappointing?"

"They offered me a job. That's the good bit, but I looked at the houses on the market and they just won't do. Want a bit of room for a pony and we really like our privacy. Lucy longs to grow vegetables and stuff."

"You should speak to the real estate agents in town here. They might know of something."

Rupert finished the second glass, took it to the sink and rinsed it out. Turning it upside-down on the side, he smiled. "Thanks for that, Christie. Have to say I envy you. This is exactly the kind of place we'd love. Anyway, should let you get back to those roses."

"No trouble at all. Go see John Jones. He has the place with the flower pots outside. Tell him I sent you." Christie walked out of the cottage with Rupert and down the driveway.

"I think I will. Great little town. No sign of high rise buildings and shopping malls."

"No. Those are things we'd like to keep out. Have a safe trip home."

Christie watched him get into his car, do a U-turn and drive off down the road. His family sounded exactly the sort of people she would sell to. If she ever sold. Not that she planned to.

22

REPUTATIONS

C hristie missed the first call from Ashley. Her phone, along with a fresh glass of water, was perched on a post near the driveway. When it finally got her attention, she sprinted across the garden, almost knocking the glass off in her rush.

"Oh, you do answer phones!" Ashley laughed.

"Well, hello to you too!"

"Thought I'd have to drive there to get a reply."

"And you would be most welcome! What's up?" Christie reached for the glass. The day was warm, with the sun almost directly overhead.

"I had dinner with Carlo Palmero last night, and we got onto the subject of you."

"I've not seen Carlo in ages. What is he doing in Melbourne?"

"Scouting locations. Some thriller he's making next year. Most likely here at Docklands, but he asked about windswept beaches. Thought of your place."

"It would be ideal actually, as long as he picks his timing with the weather. How exciting!" Christie plonked herself onto the grass in the shade.

"Fill him in personally. He has a job, if you're interested."

Christie closed her eyes for a second.

Not Europe. Not the US.

"Do tell."

"Well, your name came up about the location and he asked where you are now. Told him you've turned into a country girl in a little seaside town and he just gave me that long, serious stare he does. Eventually he said, and I quote, 'the countryside is already beautiful, it is the city that needs Christie to work her magic'. Unquote."

Christie giggled. "You're making that up. When and where?"

"Soonish. He starts shooting in a couple of days but won't need you for a week, two at most from now. Auckland."

"He leaves things late."

"No, bella. He just wants…"

"What?"

"Let's just say there is room for you in the crew, and he wants you there."

"Is my reputation so bad, Ash? He's just finding a spot for old time's sake?"

"You've been in this industry long enough to know how fickle people are. Those who know you, love you. And Carlo does, so be good and say yes. It's only a few weeks and then everyone will forget London and start throwing work at you again."

"I'll think about it."

"No, give him a call and say yes. You can decide if you want to give up on your career afterwards."

"How do you—"

"Christie. I've known you forever. Your heart is somewhere else and that's wonderful. Just don't give up because someone else messed things up. Yes?"

"Okay. Maybe. Thank you."

"My pleasure. Ray sends his love."

"Tell him I miss him. I miss you both."

After hanging up, Christie lay back on the grass to stare at the sky. Soft clouds moved ever so slowly. The enormity of the universe washed over her, tension seeping into the ground below. Once,

Christie struggled with too many contracts. Major film companies listed her, directors personally called. All it took was one manipulative man and a devious woman to damage her reputation.

Ashley was right. If she just gave up now, then Derek and Ingrid won. She would call Carlo and accept his gracious offer. Go to New Zealand and do the best work of her life. Then she would talk to Martin. Let him into her soul, past her defences. Perhaps he would see her commitment was to him and decide he needed to take things to another level. A level where their lives would be made one.

23

SAILING JASMINE SEA

Martin was already at Willow Bay when Christie arrived. He sat on the sand, sketching the boats. She watched him from the trees, drawn to his talent; his very being. These feelings he created in her were beyond her ability to put into words. Deep, profound, eternal.

"Are you planning on sailing today?"

How does he know?

Christie joined him, leaning against his shoulder as he finished the sketch, following every quick stroke of the pencil as it formed seagulls and yachts and clouds on the paper. The heat from his body radiated into hers. She closed her eyes.

"Going to sleep there?" Martin kissed her forehead. "Shall we venture out of the bay?"

"We could stay here. I could sleep, here on the sand. With you." Reluctant for the moment to pass, Christie snuggled into Martin. He closed the sketch book.

"Or, we could go sailing. Come on, sleepyhead."

With a groan, Christie moved to allow him to get to his feet, then accepted his hand to pull her onto hers. "The sun is so nice."

"Which is why we're sailing today. Within a month there'll be more rainy days than sunny. Autumn's almost on us." Martin tossed his sketch book and pencil into a backpack. "Did you bring water?"

Christie shook her head.

"If you're sailing, plan ahead. Whilst I try to keep the galley stocked, it's best to bring what you need for a trip every time. You never know if something might go wrong. Conditions can change fast. The motor might seize when there's no wind." He headed off to collect the dinghy.

"I need to learn so much." She was right on his heels.

"Yup. That's why you'll be doing the sailing. I'm coming along for heavy labour and advice if you really get stuck."

Together they dragged the dinghy into the shallows. "So I'm the boss," Christie announced with a cheeky grin.

"Hop in. You can call yourself whatever you wish."

The dinghy slid through the water easily under Martin's guidance. This time, Christie had no flutters of fear as the water deepened. A few moments later, she was on *Jasmine Sea*, grinning like a small child with a new toy. Her yacht! Martin tied the dinghy to a buoy.

"Life jackets are under the seat there."

Christie pulled two out. Martin checked she was secure, tightening one strap and kissing the tip of her nose. "You are as excited as a little kid in Disneyland. Take a deep breath and start thinking about procedures. You've been studying?"

"I have and I'm doing the test this week. Shall I raise the anchor? And what do I do if it won't raise?"

"Under normal circumstances it will. We can practice."

"But what if it really gets stuck?" Christie peered down along the heavy chain into the water.

"Bolt cutters."

"Through that?"

"Through that. Now, you're in charge. I'll jump in if you miss a step." Martin leaned against the railing, half smiling. Dark sunglasses added an air of mystery to his face.

"I love you." Christie couldn't help herself, slipping her arms around his neck and lifting herself onto her toes. For a long moment they kissed.

Then, Martin raised his head. "If you do that again, we won't be going far."

"Aye aye, Captain. Oh wait, I'm Captain. Swab the decks!"

"You're having too much fun with this." There was a suggestion of warning in his tone. Christie grinned as she went to the winch. She thought Martin chuckled at her, but then again, perhaps it was the seagulls overhead.

Almost the moment *Jasmine Sea* nosed through the narrow gap between the cliffs, wind filled her sails. Christie kept her head, systematically shutting down the engine, raising the spinnaker with a bit of help from Martin, and steering with the breeze at their backs. The yacht responded effortlessly as they left the bay far behind. Soon the land to their left was hazy and distant.

"We'll go up as far as Green Bay." From the bow, Martin raised his voice to compete with the flapping of the mainsail. "We'll be back before dark. Gives you a decent run." He clambered back to join Christie, admiring her new confidence. She handled the wheel with a light touch, as if she and *Jasmine Sea* shared some connection. "Good work. You're doing well."

"I love it. Oh, Martin, this is amazing!" Her eyes alight with joy, hair whipped back with the wind, she was a picture of happiness.

God, I love you.

Martin busied himself fetching bottles of water, just to control his urge to kiss her over and over.

He offered her a bottle, putting a hand on the wheel to let her drink. "On the way back, we'll be closer to the coast. Look!" He pointed starboard.

"Oh. Are those dolphins?" Christie stepped over ropes and under the sail to see better, leaving Martin holding the wheel. "Come and see! They are incredible."

"I would, but someone has to steer and I thought you were the captain?"

"Sorry!"

"I'm teasing you, sweetheart. Sit and watch for a while."

Christie dropped onto the deck, leaning over the side to watch the pod of dolphins. So clear was the water that their sleek bodies revealed every twist and turn.

After a while, the yacht slowed and Christie glanced at Martin. "Come on. Back to work." He held a hand out. "Time to practice changing direction and see how close we can get to Green Bay."

24

SECRECY AND INTRIGUE

D aphne stood outside her husband's office, listening to his side of a phone call. The cup of tea she carried – complete with one of her homemade double 'chocolate cookies on the saucer – could wait a moment or two, as she didn't wish to disturb what was clearly an important conversation. John was her high school sweetheart who had swept her off her feet at the age of eighteen to be his wife. Some forty years later her heart still sped up when he smiled at her. Together they'd built up the finest real estate agency in the region and, now retirement loomed, John recently turned to something he'd always avoided: dealing with large scale developers.

"But of course it will be confidential. You can trust me completely."

Whoever are you speaking with?

"If that is your preference. But, I can't promise anything until we discuss this further."

Interesting. Secrecy and intrigue, two of Daphne's favourite things.

"Yes, I can be there at three. See you then."

It was almost two-thirty according to the clock at the end of the hall. Still, he had time for his tea. Daphne popped her head around the corner.

"Tea time!"

"Oh, Daphne. Didn't hear you coming." John closed a notebook, but not before Daphne saw the words Green Bay Lookout.

Daphne frowned as she put the cup and saucer down. "Are you off somewhere?"

"Meeting a potential client. In half an hour actually."

Daphne pulled out a chair and dropped into it with sigh. "That's better. Feel like I've been on my feet all day. So, what sort of client is this?"

After a sip of tea, John picked up the biscuit. "Not sure, actually. All very hush-hush. Don't want anyone to know they are looking in the area."

"How peculiar."

"I'm meeting them soon, so need to make a quick call and finish this tea." He looked at Daphne. She smiled back. "So, I just need to make a call?" He prompted.

"Oh, of course. I have to go and box up the rest of those cookies for Christie. Thought I'd pop up after work and catch up."

"Lovely idea. I'll bring my cup out in a minute."

"Well, I'll let you make your call."

Whatever was going on?

Green Bay Lookout was partway down a cliff, accessed by a narrow, winding dirt path. Surrounded by heavy bush, it was a protected, hidden spot attracting young lovers and tourists alike. Today there were no lovers or tourists, just Ingrid and John, sitting on the only bench in the small, railed space.

"So, you see why I insist on keeping this... between us." Ingrid almost purred. An open laptop displayed an aerial shot of River's End. "People get nervous about development. Suspicious. But I understand how to calm those concerns. Help show the key people the benefits."

"Benefits? What exactly do you mean?" John was at the far end of the bench. He'd never met a woman like Ingrid. Flame red hair cropped short like a pop star. Eyelashes so long they could not be real. Even her... well, body, looked a bit unreal. Tight green dress with a tiny waist and so short, exposing perfect legs.

"My face is here, darling."

"Um, yes." His eyes shot back to hers. "The problem is I already have a client for much of this land."

"Bryce Montgomery? You know, he's such a sweetie but I went for a drive and there's not one bit of forward planning in River's End Heights. No shops or footpaths. Just great big houses with little back-yards. Yet all this space." She touched the screen. "Then, there's the demographic to consider."

"What demographic?"

"Think ahead, John. What kind of people do you want as neigh-bours? Who will bring community spirit? Money for the benefit of all home and business owners in your lovely town?" She closed the laptop and crossed her legs, leaning closer. "You need a mixture of wealthy retirees and weekenders."

"But we don't have any retirement villages and no plans for them here."

"No need. I'm talking about early, self-funded retirees, cashed up and wanting a quality home in a peaceful town. They'll bring their wisdom and friendship. As for the weekenders, well, that's where the town really benefits. Schools won't be impacted because most of the time they'll only visit on weekends and school holidays. They'll bring the real money. Spend up big and give your community a chance to grow enough to keep its current residents from leaving. Now, doesn't that sound better than a mostly empty estate that nobody really wants to live in?"

John nodded. "I'll need to have a look at what's already signed and sealed. Then we can talk further."

"Perfect. Not a word to Bryce. And not even a whisper to another soul."

"Not even my wife? Daphne is my right hand in the business."

Ingrid put a hand on John's leg and squeezed it. "In my experience, wives don't understand that sometimes their husbands have to do...

things, without them." She smiled and stood up in one elegant move. "I'm going to watch the sea for a while. Give me a call. Soon?"

John pushed himself to his feet. He extended his hand to shake but Ingrid had already turned away and stood, staring out at the calm sea. He dragged his eyes away from her and trudged back up the track.

Ingrid watched a yacht only a hundred metres or so out. Her eyesight was excellent and she immediately recognised Martin Blake doing something with a sail.

Such a good-looking man. Interesting. Intelligent. Christie once told her he had a logical mind. He did. Except, she decided, when it came to Christie, who now appeared from the lower deck carrying drinks of some sort. How much fun it was going to be taking his attention away from little Miss Christie.

Nothing personal, dear.

She blew a kiss toward the yacht.

"I think that was the best afternoon of my life and nothing will change my mind." Christie leaned back against Martin, his arms around her. They sat on the beach, much as they had earlier in the day. Tiredness weighed her down but her mind strayed to the dolphins and waves.

"You did well. A few more runs and I'll feel confident handing over the keys."

"Thank you. You were a great bosun. Don't tickle me!"

"I was a great...?"

"Teacher!"

"Better. You need to practice rowing though."

"That's your job." Christie only half joked. Her attempt at rowing back ended after Martin pointed out she was heading back to sea and took the oars again. "Captains don't row."

"I need to go collect Randall from Elizabeth."

"I bet Angus made a fuss of him. Oh, I can't wait for you to meet him. You'll come to dinner tonight? Please?"

"I don't wish to intrude."

"Now, that is something you could never do." Christie touched his face. "You are the two most important men in my life. I thought we'd just go to the pub. Let someone else cook."

"I've exhausted you."

"Not quite. So it's yes?"

Martin answered with a long kiss.

"I could stay like this." He finally admitted. "Here, with you in my arms."

"I love my life. I'm so lucky." Christie sighed in pleasure. "There's little more I could want."

"There must be more though. Work? More travel? Family, perhaps."

Christie gazed into Martin's eyes, searching for meaning behind the question. "There is a bit more I need to finish. Some work, and I'll tell you about it once I have some details. But, I don't want to be travelling all the time. Not now. This is my home. My family is here."

What was he asking? About children, or whether she had other dreams to fulfil? She'd never seen him around children. Perhaps he didn't want them, like Derek hadn't.

That was a deal breaker with Derek, along with other things. But Martin was different. She loved him with all her heart and should he not want a family, then love might still be enough.

But I want children.

She wanted to ask him what he meant, but the moment had passed.

Martin was on his feet, backpack over his shoulder, hand outstretched. "Coming?" His expression was thoughtful. Or, maybe it was just the late afternoon light.

25

ANYTHING IS POSSIBLE

E vening closed in as Martin cut across country to reach Palmerston House. The Lotus had zoomed past earlier, top down, with Christie calling out some cheeky comment with a wave. She had done so well today and he knew the decision to gift her the yacht was the right one.

He whistled as he neared the front steps.

"He's over here." From the far end of the verandah, Angus called out.

Martin grinned as he drew closer to the bench. Randall wagged his tail at Martin, but made no attempt to move from the side of the older man he sat beside. Had a friendlier dog ever existed?

"Good evening, I take it you are the owner of this rather wonderful dog?" Angus stood and offered his hand.

Martin shook hands. "Don't know about owner. He is quite happy to share himself around. Martin Blake."

"Angus McGregor. I believe we have more in common than a golden retriever."

"Christie can barely contain her excitement at us meeting. She has it all planned for dinner tonight."

"Oh dear. Shall we pretend this didn't happen?" Angus leaned toward Martin, his voice hushed. "I'm game if you are."

"I wonder how long it will take for her to work it out."

Randall whined at Martin and both men reached a hand to his head. Then laughed.

"Would you care to join me?" Angus sat down.

Randall lay down immediately, so Martin relaxed on the bench. It was pleasant to sit here in the near darkness as the trees became silhouettes. Solar lights along the driveway flickered on. The fountain randomly changed colour, a tribute to Martha and Thomas' wedding. Elizabeth had refused to let Christie take the lighting system back out after the reception, not only for the pretty effect, but as a reminder that anything is possible.

"I believe the pub is only a short walk from here." Angus said.

"Five minutes. I'd offer to drive you, but only have my grandfather's dreadful pile of junk, or an old motorbike."

"I'm partial to motorcycles. My father had a beauty that he rode everywhere. Still remember the growl it made when he powered it down."

"Mine gives more of a whimper than a growl. Perhaps walking is a better idea. Christie would be horrified if we front up on it at the pub."

"Indeed."

Martin glanced at his watch. "I'm going to take the boy home and feed him. Have you spoken to Christie about what time to be there?"

"Briefly. A moment or two before you arrived. She said she needed to get the sea spray out of her hair."

"We were sailing."

"I beg your pardon. I thought you said sailing!"

Martin chuckled. "Seems impossible. Christie had almost full control of *Jasmine Sea*, out in the open sea and back. And she swims. Not quite as confident about deeper water yet, but it's a process."

"That fear was her biggest. And sadly I let it happen." Angus dropped his head. "Instead of standing up to Dorothy Ryan, I watched a happy, self-assured little girl retreat into quietness. Becoming invisible at times."

"I've never known where that fear came from. Christie once mentioned Dorothy forbidding her from swimming in the sea, but that's all."

"After losing her parents, all Christie wanted was someone to love. In spite of her sorrow, she was such a loving, sweet child. Bit by bit, her grandmother's coldness and occasional fury taught her to rely on herself. She's good at that."

"You're not at fault. And Christie would be heartbroken if she thought you blamed yourself." Martin stood and Randall jumped to his feet. "Christie was lucky to have you."

"As she is to have you, Martin."

With a nod, Martin took his leave. After one more pat from Angus, Randall tore after Martin.

***

Christie tapped her feet on the floor. First to arrive at the pub, she'd chosen a booth at the furthest end where it was a bit quieter and had a window view of the street.

"Would you like to order a drink?" Lance, the long-time owner of the pub, laid out cutlery for three.

"I'll wait for Martin and Angus, if that's okay? Although, would you arrange a bottle of our Chardonnay please? And three glasses."

"Your wish is mine to fulfil. Do you know that they also grow olives at the winery? No? I shall also bring a complimentary plate of olives, from their own harvest." With a flourish, Lance disappeared into the kitchen.

Martin slid into the seat beside Christie.

"I didn't see you come in!"

"You were busy flirting with Lance."

"Well, my flirting got us a plate of olives. Not a bad result. How's Randall?"

"Exhausted. Pretty much ate his dinner, went for a wander, and tucked himself into bed. How do you feel after our sail?"

"Happy. I'm getting the hang of it, not that I can envisage sailing alone. I mean, why would I ever need to?"

Martin kissed Christie's cheek. "Good."

"Oh look! Here comes Angus, quick, let me out. Please." She added with a grin. Martin made space and she rushed to hug Angus.

"Angus, meet Martin. Martin Blake, Angus McGregor."

Martin and Angus met in a hug. Like long lost friends. Martin stepped back, gesturing for Angus to take a seat. "You're looking very dapper tonight, Angus."

"You too, Martin. What is that term? Ah, yes, you scrub up well."

Martin waited for Christie to sit again before joining them. "Considering how little time I've had to get ready, that means a lot."

"And how is Randall?" Angus enquired.

"Okay. What's going on?" Christie demanded. "You've already met!" Her downfallen expression made both men laugh. "Stop. You're not funny. Either of you."

"Wine for three?" Lance arrived with a tray.

"I need my own table, Lance." Christie said. "But I'll take the whole bottle with me."

"So, wine for three." He placed a platter of olives, bread and cheese in the middle of the table. "This should help."

Under the table, Martin captured Christie's hand and squeezed it. She wouldn't look at him, so he gently pulled her toward him and whispered, "I love you."

Her eyes flickered in his direction and the corners of her mouth curved ever so slightly.

The wine poured, Angus raised his glass. "To friends and family."

Martin passed a glass to Christie and they both tapped Angus' glass. "To friends and family."

"Where's that fancy car of yours?" Martin asked Christie.

"At home. I'll walk back."

"I'll walk you home."

Christie nodded. Once she would have argued that it was a safe town and she was a capable adult. The arrival of *Sole Survivor* and the odd feeling she had of not being alone last time she walked home changed that. Only a little bit. After all, it *was* a safe town and her cottage was secure. Nothing to worry about at all.

26

RECONNAISSANCE

By the light of a small flashlight, Ingrid wandered around the cottage. Why would anyone want to live here? Old, run-down place with small rooms and no walk-in robes. For goodness sake, only one bathroom. She opened the wardrobe in Christie's room, inspecting her clothes.

She has good taste.

Ingrid picked up the photograph from the bedside table. She cared little for romance, it was a ridiculous waste of energy better spent pursuing wealth. A quaint shot of Martin and Christie made her stomach turn.

The bathroom interested Ingrid, with a cabinet next to the sink and one behind the mirror. The quality and selection of make-up and perfume was impressive. Unable to resist, she dabbed a different scent on each wrist, sniffing one and then the other. She sprayed another on the side of her neck, wrinkling her nose.

In the kitchen, she opened the fridge. Not much other than cheese, wine, and fruit, but it reminded Ingrid she was hungry. On the kitchen table was a satchel. She undid the clip and peeked inside.

Her phone rang and she jumped, dropping the satchel.

"What is it, Rupert?"

"They've just left the pub. The old guy went one way. Christie and her boyfriend are walking in your direction. Looks like lover boy is going home with her."

"Then come and pick me up. I'll wait on the corner." She hung up, annoyed. Clearly this backwater town had no night life.

As she hurried down the road, she dialled Derek. Potholes and a lack of a footpath made for an uncomfortable walk in heels.

He answered almost straight away. "Anything?"

"Nice make-up and clothes. She certainly has some class."

"Ingrid!"

"I couldn't find the painting. Not in the cottage anyway, so maybe the artist repossessed it."

"You were in the cottage?"

"Well, if she's going to leave windows unlocked…"

"You're insane."

"Thanks. I'll call when I'm back at the hotel. Rupert's on his way to get me."

"Stay out of sight."

"I wish you were here. Not Rupert."

"Put up with him a bit longer."

"I can see his car. *Ciao.*"

She made it to the corner as the sedan pulled over. Cigarette smoke wafted out when she opened the door. "Put that out, now." She wound the window down, slamming the door behind her. "Kill your-self with them, but not me."

Rupert wound his own window down enough to toss it out. "How can you complain, smelling the way you do? What the heck type of perfume is that?"

Not expecting an answer, he touched the accelerator and drove away from River's End.

27

UNSAFE

A rms around each other, Christie and Martin stopped at the end of her street to gaze out over the moonlit sea.

"So peaceful. So perfect." Christie said.

"Yes."

"Except for that." Slipping out of Martin's embrace, Christie crossed to the other corner to a smoking cigarette butt. She extinguished it with her shoe, then found a tissue in her bag and picked it up. "Seriously, does nobody care about bush fire risk?"

Martin followed her and took the tissue and buried it in a pocket. "You do. Beautiful girl, you never fail to surprise me."

"I do? Surprise you?"

He kissed her, taking her hand. "Did you enjoy this evening?" They wandered down the street.

"Apart from you and Angus ganging up on me so much, I did."

"We did not. It was interesting to hear from someone else about your ongoing disregard for security. It was probably just as well your grandmother was away when you left the house unlocked, and the gate, and—"

"Okay, okay. That is enough, thank you. I was sixteen."

"Don't use your age as an excuse. I shall have to spend more time with Angus."

"He's leaving in the morning." Christie said.

Martin halted in the middle of the road and pulled her into his arms. His hands slid right down her back, pressing her against him so that she had to tilt her head back to look at him. His fingers tapped her bottom like he was playing a piano. "Is that a lie?"

"Yes." Christie's breath left her. He was not serious, she could see amusement in his eyes, but the tone he used, and the way he held her brought that heightened anticipation rushing back.

For an endless moment he watched her as mild alarm softened into desire. "Just so you know, I need honesty. Lies don't work for me."

"I know. I do know, and I was joking."

"Don't ever lie to me, Christie. Please." His face hardened.

Christie reached up to touch his cheek. "Hey," she said softly, "I'll never knowingly hurt you. Don't you know that by now?"

"Yes. But sometimes people don't mean to lie. They promise they'll be there, then..." Martin abruptly released Christie and turned away. His head dropped and his hands clenched.

Christie stepped in front of him and took one of his hands, unclenching his fingers and kissing his palm. "Martin, it's okay. My parents did that too."

He raised his eyes to meet hers.

"I'll always come home, I promise. I won't leave for long. Ever. Listen, I've been asked to go to Auckland next week for a film shoot. Just for a couple of weeks. Tell me to stay and I will."

"You want to go."

"Not desperately. But I want my reputation back and this will help. Whether I ever go overseas for work in the future is a whole different matter, but this job, well, I would like to do it."

As if forcing his body to relax, Martin drew a deep breath. "Go. Do this, because you'll always wonder otherwise."

"You're sure?"

"It's part of the package. Besides, I have a portrait to paint and you don't know what I'm like when working. I can be unforgiving of interruptions and protective of my privacy."

"Which is different from normal, how?"

Martin raised his eyebrows and reached for her but she danced away, laughing.

———————

Christie took her shoes off in the kitchen and draped her jacket over a chair. She and Martin had stood on the porch for at least five minutes, kissing and whispering. Then, just as she went to invite him in, she yawned. Another yawn quickly followed that refused to be concealed.

"Go to bed." Martin instructed.

"Alone?" She yawned yet again and he laughed.

"I think so. Sleep well and dream about the dolphins." He had given her one last long, lingering kiss.

Now, she touched a finger to her lips, smiling.

How much I love you.

Martin's new vulnerability touched her so deeply and she ached for his pain. For the little boy in him that still couldn't comprehend the accident that he alone survived.

At the bathroom mirror, ready to remove her make-up, she sniffed the air. Surely one of her perfumes hadn't leaked? She opened the mirrored cabinet and checked each one. No leaks, and now that she thought about it, the scent in the room was not specific to one of hers. More of an odd mixture.

She knew she'd unlocked the back door when she'd got home, but rushed to check it again. It was locked. The satchel left behind this morning by Angus was open, the clip undone.

You're imaging things.

She glanced inside, not that she'd know if anything was missing. Angus put it there and then she'd moved it to one side. Clipped shut. Now it wasn't.

"Oh, God."

Christie grabbed her phone and started dialling Martin. Then stopped. What would she tell him? Someone had been in the cottage? What if they were still here? Eyes wide, she grabbed a frying pan from the cupboard.

Room by room, she flicked each light on, checking behind doors and what little furniture there was. Frying pan still in hand, she tested each window. Bedrooms locked. Bathroom too small. Laundry locked. Lounge room locked. Dining room... the window yielded.

Heart in her throat, she forced the window down as far as it would go and locked it. She'd had this window open the other day, airing the room after the workmen filled it with plaster dust. How could she have forgotten to lock it?

Someone had climbed in. Played with her perfume and opened the satchel. She ran to her bedroom. Everything valuable was present, including jewellery and a small amount of cash in a box. Her passport and book of contacts were untouched.

Tonight the lights could stay on. She picked up the phone, turning it in her fingers.

Don't spoil things.

The phone went into a pocket and she checked again that the back door was locked. Disappointed in herself, Christie climbed into bed, the frying pan on the floor. Her light was off but the rest of the cottage was ablaze.

In the middle of the studio, Martin studied a part finished painting, a glass of whiskey in his fingers. The subjects were Thomas and Martha, sitting on the end of the jetty, their legs dangling and toes dipping in the sea. Perhaps they were in their early twenties. Deep in conversation, the love in their eyes reminded him of them today.

Behind them, partway along the jetty, another Thomas stared at the young couple. This Thomas was older, gripping the hand of a small, dark-haired boy. A woman walked away, toward the beach. From her long chestnut hair it could be Martha. And on the beach itself, seventy-two-year-old Thomas, on his knees, offered an engagement ring to seventy-year-old Martha.

Martin touched the face of the child. "You landed on your feet." He drank the whiskey, its warmth radiating through his body. The little boy lived deep inside him, always expecting the worst. Now, it was time to stop. Christie wasn't leaving him. Nor was Thomas.

From his bed near the window, Randall whined in a dream.

And you. Thank God for you as well.

Fatigue set in and Martin covered the painting with a sheet. Ever so gently, he woke Randall. "Bedtime." With a wag and a yawn, the dog followed Martin to the door.

In the apartment that Christie once called home, Derek prowled from room to room, listening to Ingrid on the phone. Still in the suit he'd worn all day, he wanted a shower and a shot of brandy. Tonight would offer little sleep. He had too much to do.

"Once I have John Jones in my pocket, then he'll introduce me to the right local councillors. Ones who are open to this."

"You sound confident."

Ingrid laughed shortly. "How often do I fail?"

Derek stopped at the doorway of the bedroom. His big, lonely bedroom with its king size, empty bed. Perfectly made, ready for love, the bed mocked him. "When are you coming back?"

"Do you miss me?"

"With you and Rupert away, I'm doing everything."

"Poor baby. Never mind, it will be worth it when you cut the ribbon to open the new estate."

Time for that brandy. Derek headed for the bar in the living room. "Are you still there?"

"Have you seen Chris?"

"Unfortunately, yes."

"God. She didn't see you?"

"Thanks for the vote of confidence. She was too busy cuddling up to her artist on a boat to notice anyone."

"Boat?"

"Some yacht. I was at a lookout and they happened to sail past."

"Find out about that yacht. Who owns it."

"Why bother?"

"Please." Derek poured brandy into a glass and downed it. What the hell was Chris doing on a yacht? She hated the water. Whatever hold that artist had over her, she was acting out of character. What did she see in him anyway? No money, talent, or status. To think of him touching her... he refilled his glass.

"Alright. Would you like me to take photos as well?"

"Sarcastic bitch," he said it softly. "You're doing well, Ingrid. Another few days and this will be over. Tell Rupert to up the ante."

"You mean—"

"He knows what the next step is. Now, get some sleep. I've got work to do."

Derek disconnected the call. On the counter was a folder from his solicitor. If there was a legal way to buy the land from the railway, then it would be in this report. Buying it would pressure Chris into selling her parcel of land. She would hate living beside a building site. One that he would ensure was as intrusive as possible.

He headed for the shower. One way or another he was getting her land. And although Ingrid didn't care who got hurt, he knew the moment Chris found out he was behind it, he had no chance of getting her back.

28

A GIFT FROM LONG AGO

Rain fell again overnight, finally soothing Christie into a deep sleep in the early hours. Until the rain, every sound disturbed her. The normal night-time creaks of the house and tapping of the trees on the roof became shadowy figures breaking in.

When her eyes fluttered open, it was a moment before she remembered. A moment when she smiled at the thought of seeing Martin today and catching up with Angus. Having lunch with him, invited by Elizabeth to Palmerston House. Then, realising the phone was in bed with her, it all came back.

She'd been told this town had little crime. Occasionally a break-in would occur and the locals always blamed outsiders. People passing through. Most likely and logically, that's who it was. Probably she and Martin had disturbed them when they'd arrived back. So lucky he'd been with her.

In the light of day, Christie shook off the fear. This was her home and nobody would get in again without an invitation. Her new routine would ensure she checked every lock every time she left. Martin didn't need to know her suspicions. She had it under control.

After a shower and coffee, Christie opened the satchel, inhaling the old-leather smell with a frown. Just above the clip, carved into the leather, were the initials J.O., and as Christie traced each letter, her forehead creased.

Inside, a folder and a jewellery box.

Not this again!

Her fingers trembled as she fumbled with the folder. Three photographs. The first was of herself, aged about eight, in the front garden of Gran's home. Tight plaits, a school blazer, knee-length skirt. Serious, sad eyes. A shiver ran up Christie's spine. This was the first day in her new school. A proper, private, ladies' college.

The second photo was a man and a woman, each holding one hand of a little dark-haired girl whose smile was contagious. Christie smiled at herself as a toddler, she couldn't help it. But her smile faded as she searched the faces of the man and the woman. "Mum. Daddy?" A cold stone dropped into the pit of her stomach. She turned the photo over. "With darling Christabel, aged three!"

Almost afraid, she looked at the final photograph. Her mother, so beautiful in a wedding dress, gazed at her father in utter adoration. A tear slipped down Christie's cheek, dropping onto her arm unnoticed. On the back, in different writing, "Rebecca Ryan marrying Julian Oliver. 1981."

"Julian Oliver." She touched the initials on the satchel. "Christie Oliver." She'd forgotten her real name. Gran changed it to Ryan when she adopted her. And whilst her intention was good, ensuring Christie's future was secure, it robbed Christie of her heritage. How could she have forgotten?

Nestled within the jewellery box was a heavy gold locket. She didn't need to look inside. Without even touching the locket, she remembered. As though it were yesterday.

———

Seven-year-old Christie sat on her mother's lap, playing with the locket around her neck. "It's so pretty, Mummy."

"And one day, it shall be yours." Rebecca opened it. "See? It reminds me

every day how much your Daddy and I love each other. This photo of him is from our engagement party."

"What's that?"

"That, my sweetie, is a special celebration when two people decide to get married."

"Like you and Daddy are?"

"Yes. This photo, the one of me, is a bit newer. It was taken just a few weeks before you were born. See how happy I look?"

"Is that because of me?"

"Besides Daddy, there is nobody in this world I love more. So, when you have this locket, you can see the love we have for each other, and our beautiful girl."

"When will I have the locket?"

"Not for a long, long time, sweetie." Rebecca kissed the top of Christie's head.

"You were right, Mum." Christie whispered, staring at the photographs through tears. "It was a long time."

This satchel and contents meant more than anything. In spite of the tears that kept falling, a part of Christie was back. She was Christie Oliver, daughter of Rebecca and Dr Julian Oliver. The memories rushed back, tumbling over each other. Daddy teaching her to ride a bike. Mum showing her a gorgeous sunrise. The three of them playing a board game on the wide verandah, avoiding the heat of the day.

The stone in her stomach disappeared, replaced by warmth. Love. The love of a mother and father. Happy, adoring parents. A family. It was possible to have that. It could be real.

29

CLOSE ENCOUNTERS

"I've driven around a bit, looked at those places you suggested, but none of them really appeal to me." Ingrid was a little too close to Martin for his liking. Her perfume was too strong and, up close, her make-up too thick. It was well applied but used to cover her age, rather than enhance her natural beauty the way Christie's did.

"Do you have a backdrop in mind?" He asked with a patience he didn't feel. He'd seen her keep a wide berth of Randall, who, oddly enough, had no interest in making friends.

"Somewhere typically Australian. Water, boats. You know the kind of thing."

"Koalas? Kangaroos?"

"Now you're being silly." Ingrid wandered around the studio, stopping in front of one painting, then another. "You do such interesting abstracts. May I have a glass of water?"

And a twist of lemon?

Martin opened the fridge. Did she expected the lid to be removed from the bottle as well? He left it on. Now she was flicking through his sketchbook.

"That is private." The words came out in a harsher tone than he intended and she glanced up. He held a hand out for the sketchbook.

"I'd like that place as a backdrop."

She'd left it open at Willow Bay. *Jasmine Sea* was in the background. "Not a great spot. Too much going on." Martin closed the sketchbook and dropped it on the sofa.

"Where is it? I'll go and see for myself." Ingrid opened the bottle and took a tiny sip. "This was such a good idea. I love working with real men and you, Mr Blake, have that dominant streak I admire."

Oh God, she was flirting. This wasn't going to work. His expression hardened.

"I've deposited ten thousand dollars into your account," she said. "My mother is so excited about this, so please, tell me where it is?"

Randall sat up, his attention on something only he could hear. Martin recognised that look. Christie was close by.

"If you go west past the estate, you'll find a narrow track on the left, just a few hundred metres further along."

Ingrid's face lit up. The sound of the Lotus wiped the smile away. "Oh, is that a visitor?"

"She'll wait at the house. Why?"

"I... I'm terribly private. I don't want anyone knowing I'm here." She picked up her handbag. "Is there another way out?"

"No. But if really don't want to run into Christie, I'd suggest going around the house to its left."

"Yes. I'll give you a call when I've looked at that place." Without another word, she swept out of the studio. Randall tore out of the door, heading toward the house. Martin picked up the sketchbook.

Curled up on Martin's lap, Christie's composure slowly returned. He'd put her there when the tears flowed too fast for his handkerchief to manage, cradling her in his arms as she sobbed and told him about her parents.

Now, the tears spent, Christie sat up, wiping them away with her hand. "I'm sorry."

"It's okay. You can buy me a new T-shirt." Martin lifted the wet material away from his shoulder. "Would you like to wash your face?"

"Probably."

"I'll organise some water."

Christie sprinted out of the door. It only took her a minute to rinse her face, trying not to look in the mirror at whatever damage she'd done to her make-up. Before going back to the studio she made a quick detour to Martin's room.

Back in the studio, Martin had two tall glasses of sparkling water ready. When Christie held out a clean T-shirt, he laughed and immediately stripped off the wet one. As he raised his arms to remove it, muscles rippled across his chest. Emotional as Christie was, the sight of his naked torso was distracting.

He extended his hand. "Hello. May I have that?"

"I'm thinking about it."

"Aren't you having lunch with Angus in half an hour?"

Christie reluctantly handed it over. "What would you say if I just took off my top like that?"

"Sweetheart, there'd be no talking. Maybe just a text message to Angus to cancel lunch." He tucked the T-shirt into his jeans, grinning at her expression.

She took a long drink of water, playing with the locket now around her neck.

"May I see?"

Martin closed the distance between them and opened the locket. "I can see you in them both. What a thoughtful legacy."

"I don't understand why Gran kept it from me. But mostly…"

"Mostly, what?" Martin closed the locket and placed it against her skin, taking her hands in his. "Your name? Christabel Oliver. So beautiful."

"Yes. It bothers me that Gran changed my name. As if erasing Dad. And Mum." Her eyes filled with tears again.

"Hey, don't cry. Whatever her motives, you have your name again and can use it how you wish. But, Christie, no more tears. I'm out of handkerchiefs and fresh T-shirts."

That made her laugh. "I might run home and freshen up. I don't want Angus feeling bad for bringing me the satchel."

"Do you want to come back up later? Dinner on the deck if it's still warm enough?"

"I'd love it. I might drive up rather than walk back at night."

"I'm happy to walk you home." He took her into his arms. "But just as happy for you to stay." His lips touched hers. "In fact, I'd rather you stay."

I'll never want to leave.

"Me too. I'd better get going."

"I'll see you tonight."

She picked up her handbag. "I meant to ask. Who owns the Porsche that was here when I arrived?"

"You didn't cross paths? She's the person I'm painting."

"Nice car. She doesn't have short platinum hair, does she?"

"Bright red hair. Now stop asking questions and go see Angus."

"Okay okay. I'm going. Bye Randall!" Christie waved to the dog, who wagged his tail and followed her to the door.

30

SWEET BEGINNINGS

Christie let herself into Palmerston House, expecting Angus or Elizabeth to greet her. Instead, the foyer was deserted. "Hello?"

Laughter drifted from the back of the house. Christie followed the sound down the long hallway and to the kitchen. She stopped in the doorway, unnoticed by Angus and Elizabeth. Both wore aprons and he had flour all over his. His sleeves rolled up, Angus kneaded a ball of dough.

"Now, if you will, add a little more flour and we'll roll the first sheet out." Angus put the rolling pin to one side.

"You want more flour?" Elizabeth pointed at Angus' front and they both laughed.

"One can never have enough to make quality pastry."

"Then more flour is coming right up." As she reached for the glass jar, Elizabeth saw Christie in the doorway. "Oh, hello!"

"What are you making?" Christie wandered in, sniffing rich, meaty aromas with approval. "I haven't seen you in an apron in years, Angus!"

"Beef Wellington. This dear lady has not had a traditional version since leaving England so I am making one."

"Did you know, Christie, Angus has worked in some of London's most exclusive hotels?" Flour added to the bench, Elizabeth put the jar away. "Oh, you're here for lunch with Angus!"

"We can do it another day." Christie pulled out a stool and sat down. "Besides, I'll be taking you up on your kind offer of a room this week, once Barry tells me the schedule. Angus, you are still here for a few days?"

"I might stay a little while. That is, if Elizabeth has my room free." He glanced at Elizabeth, who smiled back.

"Christie, there's a jug of my lemonade in the fridge if you'd like a glass? Angus, shall I get a tray for the pastry?"

"Please do." Angus rested his hands on the bench, his attention on Christie. "You have the locket on."

"Thank you for bringing Mum and Daddy back for me." Determined not to cry, Christie spoke slowly. "I'd forgotten my own last name. Now, I feel as though I'm more… whole, I guess."

"I am glad. That satchel was one of the last things I found as I packed up Miss Dorothy's house."

"I'd like to ask some questions. If that's okay? I just need to think a bit first."

"Whenever you wish."

He returned to the pastry as Elizabeth brought a baking tray over. They exchanged a smile. Christie got to her feet. "I might go home and leave you to your cooking."

"Do you have something at home for lunch?" Angus glanced up.

"Now you sound like Martin. Yes, I do."

"He's a wise man."

"Okay, I'll be going now!" She grinned and waved as she left. They called out "goodbye" at the same time, resulting in another laugh between them.

How wonderful!

Whether this was the beginning of a great friendship, or something more serious, they certainly both deserved happiness.

Under starlight, Martin set a small table with silver cutlery and white plates on a dark red tablecloth. He lit a short red candle and draped a few tendrils of jasmine around its base. Beside the table, a silver ice bucket held a bottle of their favourite wine. He stood back, pleased with the effect. A perfect setting for a perfect night.

"Oh, it's beautiful!" Christie stood at the bottom of the steps, her eyes wide. Martin swung around. Dressed in a blue lace dress softly following her shape, hair sleekly pinned in a low chignon, Christie was a picture of elegance. Her only jewellery was the locket, and her very high heels accentuated stunning legs.

"You are beautiful." Martin crossed to the top of the steps and offered his hand. Christie accepted, her radiant smile almost taking his breath.

At the top of the steps, she reached up and kissed his lips. "And you are so handsome. And, you smell of strawberries and the sea."

"A new candle combination? Would you care to sit at our table, or join me inside whilst I finish the entree?"

"You sound so formal! I should love to come inside."

Randall rushed through the doorway. She leaned down to kiss the top of his head and stroke his velvet ears.

"Shall I leave you two alone?" Martin offered his arm. "I might reconsider kissing you tonight."

"Why? Randall is clean," Christie curled her arm through his. "I mean, I don't know what's been in your mouth!"

"I might also reconsider sharing the wine with you, if such disrespect continues."

Christie leaned her head against his shoulder as they walked. "I'll behave. Oh, what smells so good?"

Martin pulled out a stool at the long timber kitchen bench. "You do." He dropped a casual kiss on her neck as she sat down. "As far as food goes, I've made a seafood bisque to start, followed by ricotta ravioli in sage butter sauce. Stop drooling. And something nice for dessert."

"I'm going to have to improve my skills if this is the standard you bring. May I help?"

Now in the kitchen, Martin turned the heat on underneath a large pot. "No, you may sit there and tell me about your day. And would you like a martini?"

"Full of surprises and so good-looking. Yes, I'd love one."

As Martin prepared martinis, Christie told him about Angus and Elizabeth, making him laugh at the description of Angus covered in flour.

"I've never seen Angus so happy. Oh, thank you." She took the glass. "Wouldn't it be wonderful if they got together?"

"Cheers." Martin tapped his glass to hers and they sipped. "In a previous life, were you a matchmaker?"

"I might have been. A matchmaking candle maker. Good that I only make things, not destroy them! By the way this martini is delicious." She took another mouthful, closing her eyes in bliss.

———

"Do you think there's rain coming?" Christie shivered slightly as a heavy breeze lifted the sides of the tablecloth and flickered the candle.

"Yes. Is the roof up on your car?"

"I locked it before I left. Oh, you thought I drove. No, it's at the cottage."

"That explains Randall not hearing the car. Or me. But... those shoes?"

Christie laughed. "I only put them on when I got near the house. My runners are in the bag. It was too nice not to walk and I detoured to thank Sylvia for the lovely dessert the other night. She told me Belinda is settling in well. She's in a shared apartment with three other girls and is trying to teach them how to cook."

"Best thing for her. She's sensible and keen to make you proud. Like I am." He reached across the table for Christie's hand. "You've given Belinda direction and shown Sylvia that change is okay." The breeze returned, strong enough to extinguish the candle. "If you'd like to take my glass, I'll bring this inside."

Christie followed Martin after he carefully pick up the table and carried it into the house, setting it down near a window in the living room. He went back out to retrieve the ice bucket and Christie took their empty plates into the kitchen.

"Shall I relight the candle?" she asked.

"Soon. Before it rains, would you look at something? A painting I'm doing? I'd like your opinion."

"Mine? Of course, not that I know much."

"Are you okay to get to the studio with those shoes on? Or, I could carry you." Martin offered with a grin.

Christie slipped them off. "Bare feet will do. You can carry me back if I get tired."

All the way to the studio, Christie wanted to dance, rather than walk. The wind carried the scent of the sea as Martin led her across the dark, silky grass. It was a bit surreal, barefoot before the rain.

The studio was warm. The floor-to-ceiling windows and multiple skylights allowed sunlight through from most directions and, once it was closed up, it stayed pleasant. Martin took Christie to a covered painting.

"It isn't finished and I don't know whether to keep going or discard it."

"Is it that badly painted?" Christie teased.

"It is exceptionally painted. Christie, it's the subjects that concern me. I don't wish to offend them." Half raising the sheet, he paused. "Be honest. I would prefer to destroy it now than cause them one moment of distress."

Puzzled, Christie watched him remove the sheet. He walked away, as if unable to witness her reaction. Goosebumps rushed over her skin and the fine hair on her arms stood up. "What have you done?" She whispered, eyes riveted to the most incredible work of art she'd ever seen.

31

BATTLING FOR TRUST

"You hate it."

Dismayed at the dejection in Martin's voice, Christie held her hand out. "The opposite! I am in awe, absolutely astounded by the beauty and emotion of it!"

He didn't move, his eyes on the floor. "You asked what I'd done."

Christie went to him, taking his hands in hers and squeezing them. "Yes, I did. Because you've taken life experiences and somehow... imprinted them. Turned them into something so haunting that I will not allow you to destroy it!" As her voice became more forceful, Martin looked at her. "You wanted my opinion? Okay, then come with me."

She dropped his hands, her eyes demanding he follow her, then she returned to the painting and waited. After a moment, he wandered across, stopping behind her to wrap his arms around her body.

"No more talk of destroying this. It is alive and deserves to be finished." Christie felt him relax against her and leaned back into him. "I understand your concern though, in case this might remind Thomas and Martha of times they'd rather forget. But Thomas painted the seascape of the night Martha left him, then tried to give it to her."

"True. But that was between them. This is… different."

"Yes. You are freeing them. The young lovers, the separated and heartbroken individuals, the reconciling pair. And you." Christie turned around in his arms, pulling him close. "You're freeing the little boy. He's earned freedom."

How far they had come. Once, any talk of his childhood or the dark years he and Thomas shared would result in a wall coming down between them. Now though, Martin's eyes gave away the hurt still within. But there was hope as well. "Thank you."

Rain pattered on the roof. Martin released Christie and reached for the sheet. "We'd better get back to the house."

Cold without his embrace, she rubbed her arms. "Speaking of paintings, I was in the garage today."

"We need to do something with it."

"I have no idea why I have it and I'm worried about who owns it now. Is it mine? Yours?"

"Or Derek's. Sweetheart, I don't know. We might need to get legal advice."

"Or I could ask him."

"Absolutely not!" Martin shook his head as he checked the skylights. "That's what he wants."

"Perhaps. Or it could be an apology. Or maybe he just doesn't want it."

"Then he'd sell it, make something back."

"Martin, one phone call will clear this up and then we'll know."

"And I said no." Martin went to the door and flicked the light off. "Come on, it's going to bucket down any minute."

"You can't just tell me what to do!" Christie didn't move, crossing her arms and raising her voice a little.

"I'm going to get dessert and another glass of wine. Join me or stay here, but if it's the latter, lock the door." The corner of his lips curled up. "Coming?"

The light rain abruptly became a downpour. Christie stomped across the grass, refusing to sprint but determined to stay ahead of Martin. What made him think he could just tell her what to do? If she wanted to call Derek, she could have done so without talking to Martin first.

So, why didn't you?

Ignoring her inner voice, she rushed up the steps, slipping on the top one.

"I've got you." Martin caught her before she fell. "Slow down."

Christie found herself swept up and carried like a baby. "I can walk."

"I have no doubt but if you keep wiggling we'll both end up on the ground."

Going straight through the open sliding door, Martin continued to his bedroom. At the end of the bed, still on his feet, Martin shifted Christie's body so that she had to look at him. He stared at her, one eyebrow raised, expression thoughtful. She squirmed.

"This could go a few ways."

"Why? Do you want me to stand in the naughty corner?" Christie could not help herself.

His other eyebrow joined the first.

Don't give him ideas.

"I... um, I only ever get cross with you. Nobody else really."

"Is that meant to make it okay?" He asked.

"No. It's just sometimes you make me so angry. I'm sorry." Her voice was a whisper.

Martin sighed and sank onto the edge of the bed, Christie on his lap. Water dripped from her now bedraggled and wet hair onto his arms. "Let's sort a couple of things out. First of all, Derek is up to something. Whether it is just rattling you for old time's sake, or still attempting a land grab, there's an intent behind sending the canvas. You phoning him is playing into his hands."

"You might be right. But you don't need to tell me what to do."

"Which brings us to the second thing. I have the utmost respect for

33

SEEDS OF SELLING

L eaving Martin in the morning was hard to do. Dawn found them awake, wrapped in each other's arms, discussing *Jasmine Sea*. Christie's Marine Licence exam was on Tuesday. "You know what's required, and if you forget, just think about the feel of the boat." Martin advised.

He'd made them coffee and tried to keep a stern tone with Christie about getting breakfast at home, but it was difficult when she kept agreeing with such compliance he almost laughed instead.

"I'm practising being a first officer," she'd stated ever so solemnly.

"At this rate I shall demote you to deckhand," he'd replied with a grin.

After coffee, she'd reluctantly packed her dress and heels into the bag. Not once had he suggested she stay here instead of Palmerston House. As she walked home along the beach, she wondered if her behaviour earlier in the evening had been a factor. She needed to watch her temper.

By the time Barry and his crew arrived at the cottage, Christie had moved the Lotus onto the grass verge. Today was a big one, with deliveries expected for the bathroom and laundry.

Christie unlocked the garage and went inside to stare at the box containing *Sole Survivor.*

"Morning, Christie." Barry tapped on the garage door, leaning against it to adjust a boot. "What if the boys put that into your bedroom? We'll keep the door closed anyway and lock it up at night. Probably less risk of damage than the comings and goings in here."

"Good idea. I'm all packed so it can go against the wall."

"There's something I need to ask about." Barry straightened up with a lopsided grin. "Er, it appears you already have a front door."

"Got a bit carried away with some spray paint. How long until the real one arrives?"

"Few days. But we'll open the entry way up internally first. I'll probably do that today, maybe tomorrow. Are you going to be up here at all this week?"

"I'm part way through clearing the veggie gardens, so yes, you'll see a bit of me."

"Good. Just in case I need to check anything. Looks like you've got a visitor." Barry gestured to the front of the house.

Rupert stood outside the fence in the driveway, waving.

"Interesting," Christie said. "I'll leave it to you, Barry."

———

Rupert watched Christie walk toward him, wishing his purpose here was to invite her to dinner, to New York, to anywhere really. She was one classy woman and he silently cursed Derek. He didn't care for his employer and even less for Ingrid, but the pay made up for it. This job was unsavoury, but he'd do it, and do it well.

"Hello, Rupert. What brings you by?"

"How goes the renovation?"

"Doing bathroom and laundry as we speak. Then the kitchen."

Rupert whistled. "Big job!"

"Can't wait to see the end result. So, passing through town?" Christie regarded him with those emerald eyes and he almost forgot himself.

He did his best to look embarrassed. "I wanted to thank you again for your hospitality the other day. Lucy told me I should extend her thanks as well, you know, she worries about me."

"Not necessary. It was only a glass of water."

"I went to see the estate agent. Spoke to his lovely wife, um, Daphne? Anyway, she took my details and is apparently sending some stuff through the post for us to look at together. You know, about the town and some new estate?"

"River's End Heights." The expression on Christie's face told Rupert how little she thought of it.

"Sounds right. But, here's the thing. I kind of fell in love with this place."

"The cottage?"

"I told Lucy all about it and she almost jumped up and down in excitement. Not that she did, what with bubba on the way, but you know what I mean. So, um, is there any chance you'd consider it?"

"Consider..?"

"Selling me the cottage. It'd be perfect for Lucy and the little one when she comes along. Room for a pony. Grow our own stuff and such a nice town."

Christie was quiet. She hadn't said no. But she was quiet.

"I can pay whatever you ask. We'll be selling our place in Melbourne and it's a seller's market there."

"It isn't a matter of money, Rupert. I just don't know if I want to part with the cottage. My Gran left it to me and it has a lot of meaning attached. Lots of history. Besides, there's someone in the family I've been thinking of gifting it to."

That stunned Rupert and he covered his surprise with a broad smile. "How generous! Young family?"

A beautiful smile crossed Christie's face and Rupert gulped.

"Not young. In fact, they are quite... senior. But this would be perfect for them."

"It is a bit out of town though. A bit isolated. No neighbours by the look of it, which appeals to me. But older folk, well, perhaps they like being close to amenities."

"You don't know them like I do."

Rupert patted his forehead with a handkerchief. "Well, if you decide to sell, please think of me first. Lucy and I would treat it like the family home neither of us ever had as kids."

"Yes." Christie had the oddest expression on her face, almost sad.

"The lovely Daphne has all my details. You know, in case you want to have a chat."

Christie extended her hand. "I appreciate the offer."

A truck rumbled down the road. "Better let the crew know the new bathroom is here!" Christie smiled at Rupert and hurried back to the cottage.

Rupert scowled. She wasn't going to cooperate. Not yet. Plan B time.

34

WHAT CHRISTIE LEFT BEHIND

As soon as the elevator doors opened, Derek was inside and hit the button to take him upstairs again. Hopefully, Ashley and Ray were back in their apartment and not skulking around the hallways. To think he'd once called them friends. In hindsight, it was Chris they liked. Their loss.

Derek went straight to the room they'd used as an office. What exactly was still here? The night Chris left him, she packed only a few suitcases.

He rummaged through the drawers of the filing cabinet. Some old receipts, an expired passport, airline tickets kept as mementos. She'd left a shoe box on the desk and he tipped it upside down. More receipts, birthday cards, a signed menu. Rubbish.

The bookcase had big gaps where Christie had taken her favourite novels, leaving others lying at angles. Messy and annoying. Derek propped the remaining books together neatly. He'd need to buy book-ends now. And why she'd thought a photo album belonged in the bookcase was beyond him. He grabbed it, slamming the door in his wake.

He knew what was in this album. Her life before him and without him. People he didn't know, places on sets, and randomly selected moments in time that meant nothing to him. In the kitchen, he stepped on the pedal of the bin, ready to toss it in. Be done with her.

Unless. He let the lid close as he opened the photo album.

Derek flicked through the pages. "No. Good God, what was she doing? No," then, "ah." It was a photograph of Chris with a bald, rotund man on a yacht. Ripping the photograph out, he turned it over.

Got you. Carlo Palmero.

Yes, that was the man he'd thought it was. Now, all he had to do was find out where he was filming. Or planning to film.

The phone rang, Rupert's name appearing on the screen.

"Tell me she's selling." Derek tapped the pedal of the bin again and the lid swung up.

"Sorry, boss. Not yet anyway but she's agreed to think about it."

Derek dropped the photo album into the bin. "Not what I want to hear." He strode to the entry way to get his briefcase, turning straight around to return to the kitchen. "Did she actually say she'd consider it?"

"She said she's thinking about giving it to some old couple."

"What? Damn it." Derek took a laptop out and opened it. "Then there's no alternative but to implement the next part of the plan."

"I think she's moving out today. Suitcase in the car and lots of bathroom work going on. But it's risky—"

"Then don't get caught. Or leave evidence. If that's not too hard for you?"

"Whatever you say." Rupert hung up.

The laptop booted, Derek typed Carlo Palmero into the search bar. That led to his website and a list of credits. At the very bottom was a one-line reference. "Shooting will commence on *The Devil's Dream* in and around Auckland, New Zealand, in February." Derek read it aloud. Chris was in River's End, but she had a packed suitcase in her car. Was she on her way to Auckland?

Derek closed his laptop. Just maybe there was another way.

35

A PLAN. AND ANOTHER

Martin changed into board shorts, longing to surf. He did his best thinking out on the waves with nothing to distract him save Randall's occasional complaint from the beach. Christie overwhelmed his senses and made him want to ask her to marry him.

He lay back on the bed, staring at the ceiling. Christie was moving into Palmerston House today. Instead, she should come here. Give her an idea of what life would be like when the time came. Waking up to his kisses and coffee, long days in the late summer sun, evenings filled with conversation and romance. Randall would love having her here.

I'd love it.

Surfing forgotten, Martin searched for his phone, Randall on his heels. He found it in the studio, switched off. He turned it on, then uncovered the painting in progress. Seeing it through Christie's eyes and heart, his confidence had returned.

A soft beep from his phone. Martin grimaced as he read the message from Bethany Fox. *That bay is perfect. Please meet me there at eleven. Once preliminary sketches are complete, I will transfer the next instalment into your account. Bethany.*

He'd meet her there, do some sketches and then she could go back to Melbourne and he would talk to Christie. If she agreed to stay here instead of Palmerston House, then he'd delay Bethany's painting until Christie was away.

Martin heard Ingrid before he saw her. On the phone, her voice carried along the small beach at Willow Bay in a tone of scorn. Snippets of the conversation made no sense and he wasn't interested in hearing it.

"Ridiculous and self-indulgent!" She noticed Martin and her expression changed from anger to welcome. "I'll call you back." She hung up and pocketed the phone. "Well, hello. Thought you'd forgotten me." She tilted her head, eyes hidden behind oversize sunglasses.

"It isn't quite eleven. Shall we begin?"

"Now? Oh, no darling. I'm not dressed properly and have to be somewhere else soon."

"Then why am I here, Bethany?" He crossed his arms.

"To show me the boat."

"I beg your pardon?"

Ingrid smiled sweetly and pointed into the bay. "What better place to sketch me than on a yacht, with the backdrop of the Australian bush and such a secluded little beach? Mother adores the sea and it will be perfect and so special. Just what I want."

He kept his voice neutral. "We can't just board anyone's boat."

"Of course not, how silly you must think me!" Her laugh was hollow. "As if I wouldn't do my homework. No, it is a particular boat. That one." She pointed to *Jasmine Sea*. "Your yacht, Martin."

"She is old. Not sophisticated like some of the others here. And she isn't mine anymore."

"Oh. That's disappointing." Ingrid removed her sunglasses and stared at Martin, her eyes hard. "Very disappointing. I have my heart set on this and it would be a shame to have to cancel the arrangement."

"Your choice. If, and I do mean if we go out to the yacht, it will be once only. We'll be there long enough to get the sketches I need and photographs. The rest will be done in the studio."

Ingrid put her sunglasses back on with a smile. "Sounds perfect. Let's make it tomorrow then."

"This afternoon. I'll have the dinghy ready at two."

"Anything you say." She turned to go, then glanced back over her shoulder. "It will be just us? I've told you, I'm very private."

"I can't sketch with distractions. It will be just us, Bethany."

With a nod, she wandered toward the path to the car park. Martin stared at her back, wishing he'd told her it was off.

You're being selfish. Think of Christie.

Ingrid waited until she was out of Martin's earshot and dialled Derek.

"Why did you hang up on me?" Derek demanded.

"Oh, I'm sorry. I should have continued our discussion in front of Martin Blake."

"So what happened?"

"I'm going out to the yacht this afternoon to be sketched. But apparently he no longer owns it. Was cagey about the whole thing."

"Well it's important you keep him busy. Where are you with John Jones? Shouldn't he be on our side by now?"

"We're meeting shortly and I fully expect he'll be on board. Stop doubting everything I'm doing, Derek! And maybe instead of coming up with ridiculous notions to win your ex back, you should concentrate on being ready to buy the minute we can."

"Those ridiculous notions are the last resort, if you and Rupert fail. I'd be careful, Ingrid, and do your part without telling me what to do."

"Let's not argue, particularly about a woman who left you for some deadbeat artist. By tomorrow morning, she'll be chasing Rupert, so just relax, darling."

Ingrid reached her car. She shook sand off her shoes.

"It's hard to relax with so much at stake. But you're right, arguing is pointless when we're on the same side and you're sounding jealous, which you don't need to be."

Ingrid almost dropped a shoe. "I can't wait to return to civilisation. In fact, once this is bedded down and we turn it over to the legal team, I might just treat myself to a trip to somewhere snowy, with a hot tub and brandy. Do you ski?"

Derek chuckled. "Of course."

"Well then, let's make it a date."

"When you're back, we'll talk about it. Now, be a good girl and sort John Jones out." Derek terminated the call.

She threw herself into the car and slammed the door. "Be a good girl!" she muttered. "No wonder Christie left you."

Daphne shuffled paperwork. John hadn't told her about last night's phone call and she wasn't about to ask. Trust was an unspoken part of their relationship. Whatever was going on, she had to believe it wasn't about them.

"Love, I'm popping out for half an hour." John dropped a folder in front of Daphne, frowning at her uncharacteristically half-drunk coffee and untouched cake from morning tea. "Are you okay?"

"Um, oh, I'm fine, doll. Seeing a client?" She glanced up at him. His remaining hair was freshly combed and she smelt reapplied cologne. Her heart sank.

"Just that same one from the other day. Has a few more questions."

"I remember you said they are interested in property? Maybe one of those nice homes up in the Heights would appeal?" She fished.

"Not after housing. Something a bit bigger." John kissed her cheek. "Gotta go."

"They aren't developers, are they? Because if they are, we shouldn't be speaking to them. Not unless they are with Bryce Montgomery."

Halfway around the counter, John stopped. "We're not locked in with him, apart from what we've already done together."

Pursing her lips, Daphne stared levelly at her husband. "I'm sure

"Sure I would. I can be very convincing and it's easy to prove we were alone twice recently. And the phone calls. You know, this arrangement will bring you lots of money. I mean, real wealth to retire on. Just a year of your help and then we'll go our separate ways. No need for unpleasantness."

"Get out." John picked up his briefcase. "Now."

"Oh, you will regret this," Ingrid hissed. She spun around and stomped out. When the door slammed, John put his briefcase down again and looked at his hands. They shook almost uncontrollably.

Daphne hurried to the front door when she heard the Lotus pull up. She'd been clock-watching since Rupert left. Something wasn't right, she felt it in her bones.

"Hello, lovely!" She called as Christie stepped out of the car.

"Oh, hi Daphne! Just the person I want."

They hugged.

"So good to see you, Christie." Daphne beamed when she finally released her.

"You too. Are you on your own?"

The smiled dropped. "Just for now. John's out with a new client. Why do you ask?"

"I'd like to take you out to lunch. If you haven't eaten, that is."

"How sweet and no, I haven't. But I probably should wait until he's back, if that's okay?" Daphne looked out of the door but there was no sign of John's car. "I was going to give you a call anyway."

"I can wait with you."

Daphne flopped into her seat behind the counter and Christie leaned her arms on the counter top, much as Rupert had done earlier. "Why were you going to call?"

"A young man called Rupert dropped by."

Christie raised both eyebrows. "He is certainly persistent. Did he want to look at local properties?"

"Just one. He loves your cottage."

"So he tells me."

"Are you planning on giving it to Martha and Thomas?"

"If they'll take it."

"What a wonderful gesture! You are a most generous girl and Martin is very lucky to have you in his life."

A door closed at the back of the building and Daphne's eyes widened. "That's John." She stood up.

"Daphne?"

"Out here, doll."

From around the corner, John hurried straight to Daphne and embraced her. He was sweating profusely and had pulled his tie away from his neck. He stepped back, but held onto Daphne's hand. "We need to talk."

"Whatever is wrong? You look pale. You didn't have an accident, did you?"

"No, no. I'm okay. Christie, sorry to be rude…"

"No, that's okay. Daphne, lunch tomorrow?" Christie went to the door with John now right behind her.

"I'll give you a call and arrange a time."

Christie slipped through the door which John closed, and then locked. He turned the "open" sign around.

"John?"

"Let's have a cuppa, love. There's something I need to tell you."

37

AN IRISH COTTAGE

By the light of a small lamp, Martha sat on a rocking chair in the lounge room of her cottage. Outside, dawn was a long way off in spite of spring being imminent. She loved this time of year, as the first signs of the coming season filled the air with a freshness and vibrancy unique to Ireland. With a cup of coffee in her hands and a blanket around her legs, she was warm enough. Once Thomas woke, she'd get the ancient stove going and make them both a hearty breakfast. Thomas did love to eat and yet never gained an ounce.

From here, the ever-present sounds from the ocean soothed her spirit. The waves rushing in and out were a lullaby that had sung her to sleep many times in her life. This little home had been hers for more than thirty years, bought after she'd finally decided to live out her life in the country of her ancestors. She knew everyone in the village, had taught most of them at some time or another. It was like an extended family. One she would miss so very much. The cottage had sold and, today, she and Thomas would begin packing.

"Whatever are you doing up so early?" Wrapped in a dressing gown, Thomas rubbed his eyes as he wandered in. He stopped beside Martha and she leaned her head against his side, reaching for his hand.

"I didn't mean to disturb you, dear. Go back to bed."

"Not without you." He lowered himself into a chair.

"Shall I make you coffee then?"

"Soon. Why are you sitting here all alone?"

"Just thinking and remembering some of the special times I've had here. Birthdays with friends who are long gone. Dressing the place up for Christmas and hearing the children sing carols outside, until the wind off the Atlantic Ocean sent them home in a hurry."

"There's always memories with houses. Some good and some... well, at least you'll be taking a lot of your keepsakes home."

"Yes. It's strange to think of someone else moving in. I shall probably be a little emotional at times, and I apologise in advance for any moments I may have."

Thomas leaned across to pat her leg. "Darling girl, I'll be with you for every moment. Think how much fun you'll have unpacking everything and finding special spots for your most precious things. No doubt Christie will help."

A smile brightened Martha's face. "I can't wait to see her! And Martin too."

"I just miss Randall."

Martha laughed and he joined in.

"We do need to discuss where we will live though. It's a subject you tend to avoid – see, there's the expression on your face again!" Martha said.

"There's nothing to discuss. I own a perfectly good house with stunning mountain views. What more could a woman want?"

"Well, there's small luxuries, like an inside toilet."

"There's a covered walkway to it."

"And heating."

"I've got blankets."

"Which is all very nice, but there's one thing you don't have up there."

Thomas sighed. "The sea."

She nodded, her eyes misty.

"We'll find somewhere in town, okay? Don't cry, I don't know what to do when you cry." Thomas took her hand, squeezing it tightly. "I was never going to make you live up there. We need to be close to the children."

"And Randall?" She managed with a weak smile.

"Especially Randall. Now, why don't you go and get dressed and I'll organise some coffee and kick this stove of yours into action. And you complain about my house!" He got to his feet, then pulled Martha to hers. With the lightest touch, he held her face between his hands. "I love you, Mrs Blake. If you wanted to live on that damned boat of Martin's, I'd even consider it, so never think for one minute I'll let you down."

"Oh, Thomas, I love you too and you've never let me down. Not once."

Thomas kissed her. "Get dressed. We've got a lot to do today and I want my woman properly nourished."

"You mean you're hungry." Martha laughed as she left the room.

38

AGAINST HIS BETTER JUDGEMENT

As he checked his watch for the third time in as many minutes, Martin decided Bethany was almost out of time. The dinghy was near the water line, his sketch book and camera in his backpack on its floor. She'd been on thin ice for a while and he only needed one more reason to ditch her as a client and find another way to build his nest egg.

"Hi Martin." There she was, hurrying toward him, dressed in jeans and a checked shirt. "Thanks so much for this, I phoned my mother and she is over the moon with the idea." She stopped in front of Martin, smiling. As if she was a different person.

"Let's go."

"In that?"

"In that."

Go on, refuse.

But she said nothing else, simply went to the dinghy and waited. With a sigh, he joined her.

Once on the yacht she wandered around, openly admiring the timber panels. "I like this so much more than those artificial looking boats. This has real character and you must love it! Although, didn't you say you sold it?"

"No. I gave it away."

"My goodness! What a generous man you are. Must be someone special."

"Are you ready to start? The light is good right now."

"Where shall I pose?" Ingrid was so helpful and friendly Martin wondered if she was the twin of Bethany. He directed her to the stern, where she quietly sat, eyes on the horizon. For an hour he sketched and she barely moved, despite the warmth in the air and the natural distractions of the bay.

After several sketches, Martin stood and stretched. "You've done well, Bethany. Take a break whilst I sort my camera out."

"May I use the amenities?"

"Down the steps and to the right. There's water in the fridge if you need some."

Martin put the sketch book to one side and prepared his camera, taking shots of the bay and adjusting the aperture.

"Why do you need photos?" Ingrid re-joined Martin, offering him a bottle of water.

"Thanks." He took a quick drink. "Sketching lets me get to know you. The way your face changes as you think, observe, daydream. How your hair moves. What's natural for your body. Photographs give me colour. Skin tone, eyes, your clothes. The background as well, in fact is very important, because the sketches are all about you."

"May I see?"

"No. Not until I've formulated the finished painting. Then I'll show you the process. I'm happy you've chosen to dress this way. Informal, at one with the region."

"You know, I only wear those heels and dresses because it's what I have to do in order to get ahead in a man's world."

"Let's do this before we lose this great light. There's a storm coming."

Ingrid positioned herself where she'd sat for the sketches. "I love storms. So powerful. They excite me, like a lover."

Martin ignored her, taking hundreds of images in just a few moments. Satisfied, he turned the camera off and gathered his things. "Time to go."

"Oh, good! How long before it's finished, Martin?"

"A couple of weeks. I'll start it late this week and should have something for you to look at the middle of next week. Now, do you need help getting into the dinghy?"

Back on shore, Ingrid turned on her mobile phone and immediately received a message to contact her father in England. Martin saw the panic in her eyes and agreed to wait a few moments to let her call. As she walked a little way off, talking to her father, he put the dinghy away. This afternoon her manner was so different, making it not quite a pleasure, but at least tolerable to work with her.

He flicked through the sketches, stopping on the one he favoured as the base for the portrait. She wasn't hard to draw and would be even easier to paint. Once Christie left for her job, he would download the photographs and use the best of those to select the palette.

Ingrid hurried back to Martin, dabbing her eyes with a tissue. "I am so sorry, Martin. Mother is quite unwell and my father believes she'll be moved into palliative care in a few days."

"That must be shock."

"I didn't know it was so bad or I would be back already. My next call will be the office so I can get a flight. Oh, you'll need me though, won't you?"

"Not now. Today went well and I can work from everything I've done so far. Getting to England is more important."

"Yes. Please excuse me and sorry. I'll be in touch." She almost ran back to the car park, dialling as she went.

Martin followed. He'd ridden the motorcycle up, planning to see Christie afterwards.

In the car park, Bethany leaned against her car, tears running down her face. Seeing Martin, she wiped them away as she waited on her phone. Not prepared to leave her alone and upset, he tinkered with the motorcycle. Eventually, she finished her call and found another tissue. With a soft cough, she regained her composure.

"Well, it seems I can't get a flight until Wednesday night. My secretary is trying to find something sooner, but it's how things are right now."

"You must be very worried."

"I had hoped to give her the painting when I went home. We may need to talk about shipping it instead... if there's any point by then." Her eyes welled with tears again. "Martin, what's the fastest you've done a portrait?"

"Fast enough but it won't be dry."

"I'm sorry?"

"Even if I could manage the layers without fully drying them, it will be weeks before it can be safely shipped. Oils are tricky."

Ingrid's shoulders slumped and her head dropped. For the first time, there was a vulnerability about her. She sighed deeply and looked up at him. "Well, I appreciate your honesty. It's my fault for leaving this so long." She opened the car's door.

"Bethany, wait a minute. I could do a watercolour. It won't be as vibrant or intense, but your mother will still see you as you envisaged."

Her hand went to her mouth and she nodded. "Yes, please do that. I want to hug you, but I'm sure you won't want a teary face all over your chest."

Thankful she didn't hug him, Martin nodded. "I'll start work now. You make your arrangements and we'll talk soon. I'll refund your second payment."

"You won't. I still want the oil done please, but in your own time. By the end of the week I'll deposit the balance, plus another ten thousand." Ingrid's phone rang and she got into her car to answer.

Martin started the motorcycle, wondering exactly what sort of finance industry she was in to spend such large sums of money on portraits of herself. It didn't matter. He would take care of her request and then he would have what he wanted.

39

MOVING ON

"So peaceful." Christie sat on a bench beneath a very old oak tree, close to the pond. "I'd spend all day in this spot if I lived here."

Ducks squabbled on the water and ibis stalked delicately around the reedy edges on the far side. Angus settled himself beside Christie and took the lemonade she offered.

"Did you meet my mother and father?" Christie touched the locket. "Just once."

Eyes wide, Christie grabbed his hand. "When? What were they like? Was I born?"

"One question at a time." Angus chuckled. "It was your mother and she came to visit with you. I'd only been working for Miss Dorothy for a very short time and picked you both up from the airport. You were about four, if memory serves me, and such a chatty little thing."

"I can't imagine that. Where was my dad?"

"Working, I believe. Your mother came for Miss Dorothy's birthday. The visit was cut short, unfortunately, after your mother and Miss Dorothy disagreed about something."

"They argued? What about?"

"I'm sure I couldn't say," Angus knew exactly what it was about, but telling Christie would serve no purpose. No, he remembered the day with alarming clarity.

It was the second day of Rebecca and Christie's visit, in the middle of the morning. Angus carried a tray holding tea, a glass of milk, and some small cakes into the informal living room. The formal areas of the house were off limits to children and kept in pristine condition, should visitors drop by. Not that they often did, for Dorothy had few friends.

Little Christie flicked back and forth through a colourful picture book, engrossed and chatting quietly to herself. But Dorothy stared at Rebecca with a cold expression, whilst her daughter's face was creased in distress.

"But why won't you visit us? Never is a long time, Mother."

"You made the choice to live where you do. Instead of enjoying a good life with friends and family, and a purpose, you blindly followed him to such a remote and barren place. Working amongst people who can't even pay you."

"I have a very good life, and lots of friends, thanks for caring. Julian and I love the community. It is a work of love and I most certainly do have a purpose!"

As Rebecca raised her voice, Christie looked up with wide eyes. Angus offered her his hand as he went past, hoping to remove her from the escalating argument, but she didn't see it.

"I did not raise you to live in such squalor, Rebecca! You are a Ryan, and one day you will inherit everything I've worked my life for."

Rebecca stood as Angus reached the door. "No. I am an Oliver. And I most certainly do not want or need your money. You were happy enough for me to marry Julian, so what changed?"

Dorothy also got to her feet and Christie slipped out of her chair. "As a doctor he should have put his own family first. Not the needs of... what do you call them? A community? This is your last chance to change your mind. Come home and live the life you deserve."

"What I deserve? Do you think this is it? Oh my God, Mother, you have no idea!"

As Dorothy took a step toward Rebecca, Christie backed away. Straight into a stand holding a ceramic vase which teetered, then crashed onto the floor and shattered. Angus hurried to begin picking up the pieces as Dorothy turned her attention on the child, stalking toward her, palm open.

"No!" Rebecca flew to Christie and lifted her up, away from her mother. "You will never raise a hand to my child!"

"Then get out of my house."

Angus took Christie from Rebecca and carried her out of the room. "Hush little one, Mummy is okay. Grown-ups say silly things sometimes." She clung to him, her head on his shoulder. He walked as far away from that room as he could, taking the child out of earshot.

An hour later, he drove Rebecca and Christie to the airport and waited with them as Rebecca booked a flight home. He never saw Rebecca again.

"Angus, are you okay? You're very quiet and you look sad."

"I was just remembering how beautiful your mother was, and how very much she loved you." It took all of Angus' resolve to keep those memories to himself. "There was nothing she would not do for you."

Christie's smile was enough to tell Angus he'd made the right decision.

Watercolour was the least favourite medium Martin used. It was, however, a relatively fast drying way to paint and the best option in these circumstances. If he finished it today, with drying time and proper packing it should be safe to travel by Wednesday. This wasn't ideal and, for Martin, the pressure was not welcome.

Laying out his paints and setting up an easel directed his brain to that place of unwavering focus for his subject, his job. This time though, Christie's face kept intruding. Her lips, so soft and sweet. Those emerald eyes capable of inspiration or devastation. God, he wanted her here, more than ever. All of his plans were on hold now, because he wasn't prepared to subject Christie to his moods when he painted.

He needed to talk to her, to warn her again about the tight little cocoon he wrapped himself in. To ask her to give him just a little bit of time so he could do this, and then be free to be with her. No doubt she was at Palmerston House. He'd missed any opportunity to have her here and, in reality, this was bad timing.

Get it done and move on.

Just one quick call, then he would paint.

Dusk fell as Christie drove into the cottage driveway. Barry and his team were long gone. She sighed at the inevitable mess left behind. After sweeping, she peeked into the laundry. Completely gutted, the walls had new holes cut in to provide access for the washing machine and new sink. Stepping carefully past a pile of tiles, she checked the laundry door was secure.

One by one, Christie ensured the windows were all tightly locked. Before leaving, Christie stood in the kitchen, gazing around. The place felt a bit alien now with the work in progress. Once the door was locked, Christie headed for the garage. That was secure. Everything was the way it should be.

Christie wished she was going to Martin's now. She felt alone and a bit sad. But he was painting and the slight tension in his voice when he had rung gave away his need to be alone.

Rain pattered on her windscreen as she turned onto the main road. Storm clouds loomed from the south-west. A lone yacht scurried beyond the cliffs, hurrying to its mooring. Not the night to be out on the water.

John stood at the kitchen doorway, watching Daphne stir something in a pot. She hummed, her face relaxed, as she put a lid on the pot.

"Smells good, love." He decided it was time she had a kiss.

"Oh, I didn't hear you come in!" With a big smile, Daphne opened her arms. He wrapped her up in his, squeezing her until she protested with a giggle. Then, he kissed her. A romantic, lingering kiss that left both of them a bit surprised and breathless.

Red-faced, Daphne wiggled away. "My, oh my, John Jones! It's got terribly hot in here all of a sudden."

"Well, I should cool you down with a nice bottle of red."

"But it's only Monday."

"You get the plates and I'll get a bottle."

Daphne dabbed her forehead with a tissue, then gave the pot one more stir, replaced the lid, and turned off the flame.

John wandered back, reading the label of the bottle he'd selected. "Think this will do. Been keeping it for a special occasion, and today fits the description, don't you think?"

"I think you are the most wonderful man in the world."

"Then let's open this baby and drink to us."

While he found a bottle opener, Daphne filled two plates with stew and added a bread roll on each. Instead of their customary dinner in front of the television, she rushed into the dining room and set the table. John appeared behind her with the plates. "You sit down, I'll get everything."

"First..." Daphne opened the glass cabinet and found a pair of crystal glasses, the good ones they kept for entertaining.

After John filled their glasses, they clinked them in a toast from him, "To the best darned real estate agency in the world!" which resulted in more giggles from Daphne.

For a few moments they ate in silence, then Daphne sighed and took another sip of wine. "I truly cannot understand what that woman was thinking. As if I would believe for one minute that you would stray."

"She's used to getting what she wants and I just hope she's gone for good. The trouble is she's nosing around all over the region and, before long, just might find someone who doesn't see through her."

"Should we warn the others?"

"Don't see how we can, love. Not without the risk of a law suit, should she get wind of it. She's good though. Very clever at getting a person to see her vision, and it's not a bad vision."

"Just a bad woman. Well, doll, you saw through her and sent her packing back to Melbourne." Daphne stabbed a piece of potato as if it were Ingrid.

John put his hand on hers. "If you hadn't reminded me how much we owe Bryce for his loyalty, then I might have signed something and got us into a lot of trouble. I just want to be sure we'll be comfortable when we retire."

"You did nothing wrong and you never would have. Now, tonight is special and we're going to stop talking about horrible women and start talking about helping Bryce with his next endeavour!"

John smiled and nodded. Talking shop was never old with Daphne. Telling her about Ingrid's attempt to intimidate him today reminded him why he loved her so much. Ingrid was gone, and, like Daphne, he hoped it was for good.

40

MOMENTS OF HAPPINESS

"Good God, I am happy to be back." Ingrid sank onto the sofa in Derek's office. She considered taking off her shoes, but Derek was touchy about things being out of place, so casually draped one leg over another instead.

Through the floor to ceiling windows, Melbourne city stretched out below, lights defining the buildings. A sprinkle of rain dotted the glass, but not heavy enough to spoil the view. Derek brought over two glasses of brandy. "Here, you deserve this."

"Yes, I most certainly do, being sent to purgatory for all this time."

"I would have thought Martin Blake would appeal to you."

"He does in that primitive, alpha sort of way. But he'd get tiring quickly, so no need to worry." She smiled very sweetly, then tasted her drink. "This is nice. Civilised. But I thought you wanted me to stay there longer?"

"Not tonight. The best thing is you being very visible here, just on the off-chance anyone suspects your involvement."

Ingrid covered a yawn. "Sorry, darling. I'm tired. I'll just come home with you and that way I'll have a perfect alibi." She glanced at Derek through partly closed eyelids, a tiny curve on her lips.

"Nope. We're off to the casino. Between dinner with friends and then a move into the gaming rooms, you'll be safe from any accusations. Don't pout. Go home and have a shower and I'll meet you there in an hour."

"Fine, but expect me to drink a lot of very expensive champagne." She leaned over and touched her lips to his. "It's been hard work dealing with those idiots and if I must go out, then I shall do so in style."

She started to get up, but Derek's hand whipped to the back of her neck. "I expect nothing less." He pressed his mouth against hers, forcing her lips open in a fast, hard kiss. "This will be over soon. Then we'll book that trip to the Alps."

Elizabeth suggested a game of Scrabble after a delicious dinner served in the kitchen. Angus and Christie looked at each other and groaned aloud.

"Well, what about cards then?" Elizabeth frowned.

"No, it's a great idea! We love Scrabble but we are so competitive and nobody else ever wants to play." Christie explained. "Angus is the king of unusual words and I like to make things up to delay everything whilst somebody researches to prove me wrong."

"Well then, I'm sure you won't mind me joining in and seeing what I can learn." There was a suspicious glint in her eye.

Half an hour later and trailing behind them both, Christie shook her head. "Always the quiet ones."

"Sorry, dear?" Elizabeth laid out a particularly difficult word and Angus sighed.

"Nice to see we're teaching you something." Christie grumbled.

"Care for a glass of sherry? Or wine perhaps, I seem to remember you enjoy the local Chardonnay. It might help." Elizabeth actually giggled and Christie caught Angus gazing at her with the softest of expressions.

"I'll go and find alcohol for us all so that Angus and I can drown our sorrows." Christie headed for the kitchen. Laughter drifted behind her, and she smiled. She found a bottle of wine, a beer she thought Angus would like, and glasses.

Back in the living room, she put them on the table. "Is it my turn yet?"

Angus stood with a bit of effort. "Go, see if you can complicate the situation! I believe I am now coming last."

"Shall I take it easy on you?" Elizabeth asked with a deadpan expression.

"Yes. Yes, I believe that is an excellent idea." Angus spoke with such resignation that Christie and Elizabeth burst into laughter. He handed them each a glass of wine, opened the beer and offered a toast. "To f-r-i-e-n-d-s."

"Ooh, yes!" Elizabeth added, "to g-o-o-d-t-i-m-e-s!"

"Which leaves me to toast to m-e-w-i-n-n-i-n-g." Christie grinned.

"That's not how you spell Elizabeth." Elizabeth stated.

"But it's how you spell success!"

Angus took his chair again. "In that case, I shall try this word and you may both try to spell it!"

Christie overflowed with happiness. All that was missing was Randall and Martin to have made the evening perfect.

Martin put down his brush. His watch was in the house and he refused to keep a clock in here so had no idea what time it was. He tried to focus on the watercolour but exhaustion tricked his vision. Too many versions already ripped in two, until he'd spent a few minutes scratching Randall's tummy, letting the gentle wag of his dog's tail soothe him. In a better frame of mind, he'd finished the portrait in a few hours.

He knew what the problem was. Bethany Fox being on *Jasmine Sea*. Self-reproach bubbled just below the surface. Instead of controlling the situation, he'd been too concerned about money to keep his integrity, which annoyed the hell out of him. Never again. Instead of worrying about having enough in the bank to cover every future contingency, it was time to trust himself. Trust these hands that didn't fail him. Trust Christie to love him no matter what.

This could stay here and dry overnight. In the morning, unless there were serious flaws, he would call Bethany about collecting it. Whether it would be fully dry was another matter, but he'd worked with a light touch. Cleaning up the brushes, all he wanted was sleep in soft sheets and drift into a dream as the rain tapped a lullaby. If Christie was here, it would be perfect.

Before turning off the lights, he took a moment to look at the oil he'd shown Christie last night. As if she understood exactly what his vision was, she'd got to the heart of it. Nobody in this world instinctively knew him, yet she had from the very first moment.

"Bedtime, Randall," he said. A very sleepy dog reluctantly got up, stretched, then padded out. The rain was heavier now and Randall dashed for some bushes before catching up with Martin at the house. Something made Martin close and lock the sliding door behind them. He was accustomed to leaving it open, but it was beginning to feel hypocritical to be on Christie's case all the time about locking doors, yet not bothering himself. Once she lived here, he'd insist on more security, so he might as well start now.

By two a.m. the short-lived storm had moved on and the rain slowed to a drizzle. Cold and stiff from sitting for several hours, Rupert dragged himself out of the car. He'd parked it close to the railway station, backed up into bushes right off the road where he could keep an eye on the cottage.

He grabbed a short crowbar and a pair of gloves from the car boot, then trudged through the muddy ground, past the desolate station and down the cottage driveway. During his visit this morning, he'd scoped his target areas. This wasn't about damaging the cottage, more about scaring Christie. He felt sick about it. She was nice.

He circled the cottage, flashing a narrow light through windows, stopping at the sight of the box in Christie's bedroom. The painting. It was Rupert who'd packed it up and got it shipped here, following Derek's instructions.

Inspection done, Rupert rattled the garage doors. Locked. He slipped one end of the crowbar between the doors and twisted it from side to side until the old lock gave. He pulled the doors closed behind himself.

A few boxes were open. A beautiful clawfoot bath became the first casualty with a few hard swings of the crowbar. Shards flew in every direction, one hitting Rupert's cheek.

"Goddammit!" He dropped the crowbar, grabbed a handkerchief from a pocket, and cautiously wiped blood away. Once the bleeding stopped, he retrieved the tool, angry. More careful now, he wrenched the door off the dryer and the lid from the washing machine, knocking some huge dents into each appliance for good measure.

He ignored the enclosed boxes. Instead, he uncovered a container full of accessories. Fittings, wall mounts, screws. Lifting it high up, he turned it over, spilling the contents right across the floor. That would do. Enough damage to put fear into someone living alone.

Outside, he leaned against the doors and lit a cigarette with shaking hands. His face hurt. She didn't deserve this, the woman with emerald eyes. No matter what she'd done to Derek, it was becoming a joke. No more. From now on, he'd find a way to avoid this sort of job. That resolved, he tossed the butt away and left.

———

From across the gaming room, Derek contemplated Ingrid. She might have been tired in his office, but a decent meal and copious champagne had revitalised her. She was stunning in her tight short dress and stilettos. Red hair suited her. Men wanted her and women wanted to be her. Pity she wasn't a little more... amiable. Still, she had her purpose and was an asset.

The small group she was in split up but one man stayed, leaning very close to her, his body language clear. Ingrid smiled and whispered something in his ear, her hand on his arm. He pulled back abruptly with a scowl. Without looking back, Ingrid tottered across to Derek.

He met her halfway. "Having fun? Making friends?"

"Stupid, bad smelling—"

"I get the picture. You can't expect men to leave you alone. And anyway, you enjoy leading them on, only to kick them in the guts on whim."

"Right. I think there's a compliment in there. So, can we go yet? I'm finally done with champagne and have a lot to do in the morning."

"It is the morning. Almost three actually and yes, we can leave." He lowered his voice. "Rupert just called and it's done."

"Then we've got to be ready to move. Is he back at his motel? I might call him."

Derek took her arm. "Let's go. Let him be." They sauntered out, making sure they spoke to acquaintances on the way. "We'll have breakfast at seven, okay? Go home and sleep and then we'll work on the next move."

She curved her lips. "Who needs sleep, darling?"

"I do. Actually, so do you. Thank me in the morning."

He could never tell if she was amused or irritated when he rejected her, not even after all this time. But he knew she loved being kept at arm's length until it suited him. She loved it.

41

SHATTERED TRUST

The Marine Licence test was booked for eight-thirty, just as VicRoads opened for the day in Green Bay. Although she'd studied and practised, Christie couldn't sit still as she waited, jiggling her feet until the woman behind the counter glared at her. Martin had sent her a text message just after dawn. *You'll ace this, sweetheart. Call me when you're back.*

She'd switched the phone off after sitting down. This meant so much to her, not just for the yacht but as a measure of how far her relationship with the ocean had improved. Deep water still scared her so very much, but now she had techniques to distract her from thinking about it too much. Of course, when Martin was around, he was all the distraction she required.

"Miss Ryan?"

Christie jumped up. A man beckoned from a door to one side of the counter. This was it!

The insistent ringing of his phone stirred Rupert from a deep sleep. He pushed it away and the noise stopped. He turned over, dragging blankets with him. It rang again. A bleary glance at the bedside clock reminded him Derek wanted to do a conference call with Ingrid at seven. Two hours ago.

"Okay, okay."

"I've rung you half a dozen times, Rupert!"

"Man, I've had hardly any sleep. I'm awake now."

"You've had more sleep than me, so pull yourself together and listen. You get yourself ready from a call from Christie, or the agent. If you don't hear anything by this afternoon, go and find out why."

"Huh? Like just rock up at the cottage? Hey there, Christie. So, feel like selling now I've smashed your stuff up?"

"Just remember who pays your wage." The steel edge in Derek's voice cut through the last bit of sleep haze.

"Yeah, dude, I know." Rupert swung his feet out of the bed. "Sorry, boss. Just damned tired."

"Have a shower, have some coffee. But make sure your phone is charged and with you every minute. Hang around town. Get the gossip. You'll find an opening if it comes to that but this is the best chance we have to strike."

"Will do. I'll come up with something. Maybe I can go help clean up."

"Yes, take her some chocolates. Be careful, Rupert."

"I'm not stupid. Is there anything else?"

"I'll be waiting for your call." Derek hung up.

I'll be waiting for your call.

"Don't hold your breath, boss."

Christie drove into her street, still buzzing at passing the test. Her heart jumped seeing a police car on the verge outside the cottage. She pulled over, grabbed her bag, and almost flew down the driveway. The garage doors were propped open and Barry's team stood around, looking in. Was Barry okay? Her legs wouldn't carry her fast enough.

42

A CHANGING FUTURE

By the time Christie and Martin reached the garage, most of the mess was cleaned up. One of Barry's men sifted through a pile of screws, parts, and small fittings. Another inspected each appliance for damage. Barry frowned as he tapped on his iPad.

Christie hesitated at the door. The clawfoot bath was beyond repair, its porcelain and acrylic interior shattered and the feet broken. With massive dents in the washing machine and dryer, and parts ripped off, they too looked destined for the scrap heap. She watched Martin speak to Barry as if from a great distance. Her stomach churned and, in spite of the warm sun, she shivered.

I can't lose you.

Christie covered her mouth to suppress a sob. Tears threatened and she slipped away. Through the open gate in the back garden, past the vegetable beds, running until she dropped onto the grass beneath a fruit tree.

She closed her eyes and let the silence wash over her. Christie concentrated on each breath, following its path through her body until gently exhaling. She curled her fingers into the long grass, connecting to the earth through their soft strands. Bit by bit, the panic retreated. Her eyes opened. From here, the back of the garage was just visible behind trees. If she listened carefully, voices drifted across.

She'd have to go back. Talk to Barry and find out what to do next. Move back in for a start, to prevent this happening again. Except, it hadn't stopped someone entering the cottage, touching things, spraying her perfume. Was someone watching her? Was this Derek's doing?

Arms tightly wrapped around herself, Christie thought it through. One quick phone call. Why did you send the painting? Five minutes conversation for peace of mind about the break-in. Martin said he'd handle it, but sending a solicitor's letter might not get the answers they needed, if any at all. With Martin already upset with her, what difference would it make?

The shivering returned and she held herself more tightly.

He'll understand.

She knew it wasn't true. Tears trickled down her cheeks and she buried her head in her arms.

Martin searched the cottage for Christie. Her handbag sat on the kitchen table, but no Christie. When she'd told Trev someone might have been in the cottage, anger and fear flooded him. What if she'd walked in on them? No more coming home at night alone. Hell, no more living here.

He followed the path to the orchard. His gut felt like he'd been kicked ever since realising she was still holding herself back from him. Trust and respect. With them, they could face anything together. Without them… well, the thought scared him.

There you are.

Under the tree, arms wrapped around her drawn up legs, her head rested on her knees. Martin caught his breath. He wanted to kiss and comfort her, and paddle her behind all at the same time. Get through to her that she never had to fear losing him. She was not his follower

43

AS PIECES FALL INTO PLACE

I ngrid detested the inevitable mess the wind made of her hair and make-up if she drove with the top down. It was bad enough returning to the backward little town without having to make herself presentable the moment she arrived. Instead, she played classical music and had the air conditioning turned up high.

Just after Green Bay, the Porsche caught up with a familiar, much slower sedan, cigarette smoke wafting from the partly open driver's window. Ingrid dialled Rupert. Twice, because he clearly didn't want to talk to her.

"What is it?" He finally answered.

"For a start, get that pile of junk out of my way."

"Go past."

"If you hadn't noticed, there are hairpin corners all the way along here."

"And?"

"And you are forgetting your place. People like you are dispensable." She almost spat the words.

"Oops. Sorry, ma'am. Was there any other reason for the call?"

I'd like to run you off the edge of the cliff.

"Why are you going to River's End? Has she called you?"

"No, Christie hasn't, but I expect she will. Might as well be close by to seal the deal. And why are you here?"

If anything, the sedan slowed even more and Ingrid continually had her foot on the brake. "God, can you go any faster? And what I'm doing is none of your business."

"Well, it sure was nice catching up then."

"Wait." Ingrid scowled. "If you're going to be in town, I might have something for you to do. Later."

"I'm shocked. Remember I'm happily married with a bubba on the way."

"Remember I'm behind you and just might give in to my desire… to see the back of your car sinking under the waves. No woman in their right mind would marry you, Rupert, let alone have your devil-child."

He snickered. "You know you want me. Hey, you're a bit too close. Back off, okay?"

The road forked and both cars took the left turn, off the Great Ocean Road. "You go do what it is you do. I'm going to see Martin Blake and stir things up. In the unlikely event I fail, you might need to repeat last night's events, but in his studio."

Ahead, the River's End sign signalled a reduced speed limit. If Rupert drove any slower, his car would stall. They passed the road to the cottage, then went down the hill to town. "Are you there?"

"Damaging whitegoods is one thing. Valuable art quite another. If I got caught—"

"Well, don't. His ridiculous scribbles cannot be worth much except to hurt him. If I have to, I'll chase both of them out of this town."

"I'm stopping just up here. Do you want to continue this face-to-face?"

"Are you insane? Just keep your phone on and let me know if you hear from her."

"From Christie? I dare you to say her name."

Ingrid jabbed the disconnect button. The sedan indicated and pulled into a parking spot near a bakery. She drove past, ignoring Rupert's wave and turning onto the road to Martin's house.

wrong, just commissioned a painting."

"Why? What is your motive? If you're after—"

"What do you think your little princess will do when she finds out we're involved?"

"She won't believe you. Remember, Ingrid, she's seen you in action before."

"And look what happened. No more engagement, or apartment, or career. I have a way of getting what I want."

"Get out." Martin grabbed the box and forced it into her arms. "Leave."

With a shrug, she walked away. At the door she paused and looked back with a smirk. "She was never yours and before this week is through you'll have lost her. Her place is still with Derek, as pathetic as it is."

Martin strode across the floor but she slipped through the door and disappeared. He slammed it behind her and dropped into a squat, hands pressed against his eyes.

Almost turning an ankle on the grass in her hurry, Ingrid swore and took off her shoes. How had he worked out her identity? Thank God Derek had insisted she spend last night in the city. No way to pin the break-in on her. No, she was safe – at least, once she got to her car she would be. For all she knew, he might set the dog on her.

At the gate, she glanced back. Damn him. Damn Christie and, mostly, damn Derek. She didn't want him, but she hated losing. Anything.

With all her strength, she threw the box toward the cliff. It hit the ground with a satisfying smash and bounced almost to the edge. She wanted to kick it over, send it into the ocean to rot. Except now she could hear the Lotus.

Flying into her car, Ingrid prayed she could get to the fork before Christie did. No point making things worse for herself at this point. Throwing it into gear, she forced the accelerator down.

CHRISTIE WAS RIGHT

The Porsche approached Christie as she headed to the turnoff. Before she was close enough to see the drive, the other car took a sharp turn and accelerated past Palmerston House.

Now what? She could hardly follow. For a second, she imagined the two sports cars in a thriller, a movie where she was hunting down the criminal.

Another time.

She continued toward the cliff top instead. There were things Martin needed to know.

She parked, got out, and locked the car. Never again would she fail to lock anything. That was one of her resolutions. Inside the gate, her eyes, as always, wandered to the vast ocean. It felt like ages since she'd been down on the beach for more than a shortcut. Randall barked, taking her attention. He galloped across the grass, tail high with excitement and she met him halfway.

"Hello, gorgeous boy." She stroked his velvet ears when he finally stopped circling her. "Where's Dad?"

"Don't know about 'Dad', but I'm here." Martin called.

Christie and Randall almost ran into him as they went around the corner. He steadied Christie then, holding her arms, studied her face.

customary messy bun and a flour covered apron, Sylvia was just...
Sylvia. Unless it was because Barry Parks was overseeing the
renovation?

"Daphne?" Sylvia interrupted her thoughts. "I said I'll be back in an
hour if that's enough time?"

"Yes. Yes, of course. I'll just let John know and then I'll pop to the
house. Shouldn't take long at all." Daphne moved the boxes to her
desk. Wouldn't want someone coming along and taking them. There'd
been quite enough crime for one day in the town.

Daphne hummed as she hurried to her front door, keys in hand. How
thoughtful Sylvia was, and even John surprised her by offering the
beer before she got the chance to ask. Such a lovely community and,
in reality, so safe. Whatever happened last night at the cottage was
some anomaly. Thrill seekers passing through.

As she inserted the key, she was sure she heard a thud. Surely, it
wasn't from inside her house? She giggled at her silliness and turned
the key. The door opened with the slight squeak John hadn't got
around to fixing.

Thud.

She jumped. Heart racing, she peered down the hallway. "Hello?"

Silence. Then the back door clicked shut.

Daphne let out a small squeal.

Hand on the door knob, she listened. No more sounds. She
grabbed her phone with shaking hands and dialled John's mobile.
"Come on, come on."

"What did you forget—"

"John," she whispered. "There's someone in the house."

"Daphne? What did you say?"

"Well, I think they've gone, but someone was here." She tiptoed
down the hallway.

"Did you say someone is in our home? Where are you?"

"In the hallway. I'm going to see."

"Get out of the house! I'm on my way."

Daphne stopped at the dining room doorway and turned on the light. Every cupboard door was open. All of her precious crystal glasses and the china dinner set from their wedding were shattered on the dining room table.

"Oh my."

"Daphne, are you out of the house yet?"

With a bloodcurdling scream, Daphne dropped the phone and ran down the hallway toward the kitchen.

In the fourteen years Senior Constable Trevor Sibbritt had protected River's End, he could only recall a handful of crimes. A couple of shoplifting attempts from misguided kids, arrests for drunk and disorderly, and some angry neighbours. Nothing serious. He liked it that way. An orderly town meant a happy town, and River's End was the happiest place he'd ever lived.

At first, the events of the night added some zing to his otherwise ordinary routine. An average day saw him direct traffic around errant sheep, check in on several more isolated residents, and give safety talks at the schools in the region.

A real case reminded him why he'd become a police officer and put an extra spring in his step. With the new information about an outsider going under two names with intent to deceive and probably more, he was ready for the challenge of finding out exactly what her involvement was – if any – with what he'd nicknamed the 'Cottage Job'.

The discarded painting put a whole new spin on things and he'd called in forensics from Warrnambool to take a look. Well, they were going to be busy because now he was standing in the middle of another crime scene, this time in River's End Heights.

Alerted by a silent alarm installed in the new house, he'd arrived with sirens blaring, ready for action, his patrol car abandoned across the driveway. The front door was wide open, but there was nobody home. No perps. Nothing but what looked like a small explosion inside.

Somebody had had a lot of fun. The new owners had begun moving in and their wide screen TVs, whitegoods, and glass coffee table were smashed. "What is it about frigging whitegoods?" he'd muttered as he stepped over broken glass.

He took lots of photos, expecting backup from Green Bay any minute. Then the phone rang. At first, he couldn't make out any words because the man on the line was screaming.

"You've got to slow down. Who is it?" He tried twice before he got a coherent reply.

"It's John Jones. You've got to get to my house! Daphne is there with an intruder and I think he's killing her!"

The line died and Trev almost dropped the phone.

Not Daphne!

There couldn't be a murder in River's End. Not on his watch.

Daphne ran like she had never run before. Bursting through the back door, she'd caught a glimpse of a man two gardens over. Jumping awkwardly into the third garden, he'd disappeared, but she knew where he was going. The road up to the mountains passed by the end of hers. She doubled back through her house and took off to the end of the street.

She felt for her phone. Darn. It was on the floor in the dining room.

With my precious things.

Forcing the image of the destruction away, Daphne put all her energy into getting to that corner. Each step was torture in her unsuitable shoes. Nothing had ever encouraged her to go much faster than a brisk walk on a cold day, but now she wanted to catch that man. How dare he step foot in her home!

Sweat poured down her face and her breath heaved in and out as she counted. Four houses to go. Three more. Two. There was the corner. And… wheels squealing, a dark blue sedan sped away. Daphne stopped, gasping for air, desperately disappointed.

"Daphne! Oh my God, doll!" John yelled from the other corner. He ran across without looking, straight to Daphne, and flung his arms around her. They grasped onto each other. "I thought… I though he killed you." John stammered.

Pulling herself away to look at him, Daphne's mouth fell open at the tears on his face. "No, love. I'm okay." She kissed him. "Don't cry, love. Please don't." She reached into his pocket and found a handkerchief, using it to dry his eyes. He took it from her and blew his nose.

Sirens wailed close by.

"Is that Trev?"

"I thought you were being murdered."

"Oh. I dropped the phone when I chased him."

"You did what?" John stared at Daphne with open admiration. "Did you see who it was?"

"No. But there would have been a murder if I'd caught him!"

John took her hand and they hurried back to the house, arriving at the same time Trev screamed to a halt outside the house. He leapt out of his car with an expression of utter relief when he saw Daphne. "Daphne! You're okay!"

"I couldn't catch him, Trev. He took off toward the mountains in a dark blue big car. You might catch up—"

"Don't touch anything!" Trev dived back into the patrol car, and with sirens blaring, did a U-turn.

John turned to Daphne, still holding her hand. "We might go and see what he took."

"I don't think he stole anything."

"What makes you say that?"

"He's a vandal. Just… breaks things." Her voice faltered.

"What things? Doll? Do you want to stay outside?"

Yes, she did, but no way was she letting her husband see that room alone. Chin up, she led him back into the house.

CHANGES AHEAD

Deep in bushes behind an empty house, Rupert watched the patrol car speed past. Thank goodness he'd spotted this driveway before running out of options. He was done. No more risking himself for his selfish employers. Things were getting hot in town and he was sure that woman saw his car.

He nosed back onto the road to River's End, worried he'd see the police car in his rear vision mirror. Ingrid had promised him empty houses. The front door opening and Daphne calling out had almost given him heart failure. Another few seconds and he'd have been heading for jail now.

He retraced his route as far as town, then took a right past the jewellery store. The old man who owned it sat on a bench outside. George. According to Ingrid, George virtually ran local council, so why she hadn't targeted him was a mystery. Martin Blake came out of the store and sat beside him.

He followed the track to the car park at Willow Bay, cursing when he saw the Lotus. What the hell was she doing here? And he couldn't just turn around because the top was down and Christie was in the car. As he parked, he pushed the small crowbar and balaclava under his seat.

Christie stared at him from the Lotus. No smile, a worried crease marring her pretty face. Her hands were on the steering wheel but the motor was off.

"Christie, I'm so glad I found you!" Rupert's tone of sympathy helped him fake a smile. "Someone said they saw you go this way and I just hoped you might be here."

"Who did?"

"Dunno, someone in town. I heard about that awful break-in at the cottage this morning. Wanted to see if there's anything I can do to help? I've got a mate who sells whitegoods and stuff. Get you some replacements."

"That's kind, Rupert, but no need. How do you know what happened? I thought you were back in Melbourne."

Rupert shuffled his feet. "Starting the new job next week and I'm still looking for a home for us. Too far to commute and don't want to be away from Lucy for days at a time. So, I thought I'd take another look in that new estate and see if I can talk her into something."

"Did you find anything?"

"Still have our hearts set on that cottage of yours."

"In spite of someone breaking into it? Aren't you worried about leaving your family up there alone?"

"My dad will move in as well. We'll get him a granny flat once bubba comes. So, what do you say?"

"What happened to your face?"

His hand flew to the cut on his cheek. It was bleeding again. "Shaving accident. Embarrassing really. So, will you sell to me?"

Christie started the motor. "I'll think about it."

"That's wonderful! So, you'll let Daphne know?" He stepped back as Christie put the Lotus in reverse.

"Sure."

He watched her until the Lotus rumbled out of sight. At least he had something for his masters. Damn them though if they were going to get him to do their work anymore. And nobody was going to pin those break-ins on him. He pulled the crowbar out and spent a few moments wiping it clean with the balaclava, then tossed both into the bushes.

———————

Trev drove back to town, disappointed he'd lost the car. Ahead of him, a mid-sized sedan turned from a side road and drifted across its lane. The car was green, but the driving was erratic enough for Trev to put his lights on. Maybe in her panic, Daphne had got it wrong.

The car pulled over, almost straight into a ditch. Parked behind it, lights on, Trev climbed out and, hand on holster, approached the driver's side. The door flew open and a woman stepped out.

"Hold it there, ma'am."

She froze, hands in the air and horror on her face. Trailing from one hand was a road map, which she dropped. Trev watched it float to the ground, then he glanced back to her face. Tears streaked down her face, making gorgeous blue eyes puffy. Blond, shoulder-length hair was unbrushed, and her dress might have been slept in.

"Hey, lower your hands," Trev relaxed. "Are you okay?"

"I'm lost, officer."

"Then let's get you going in the right direction. Where are you headed?" He scooped up the map and offered it to her. Up close, she was pretty, really pretty, but so upset. "What's your name?"

"Charlotte Dean. I'm so sorry, I wasn't driving very well, was I?" She took the map.

"Just don't try reading maps and driving at the same time. Okay?"

She nodded. "I'm looking for Palmerston House."

Trev smiled. "I'm heading that way, so you follow behind and we'll get you there. Are you fine to drive?" Charlotte clearly was no threat to River's End, apart from her driving.

"Thank you…?"

"Senior Constable Trevor Sibbritt. Just Trev will do. Right then, I'll go in front and we'll have you there in no time."

He waited for her to get back into her car, then returned to his. At least he'd be able to help one person today. As for the rest of the problems, well, only time would tell.

50

PEP TALK

A ngus met Christie on the front steps of Palmerston House. "This town is not nearly as quiet as you told me! The kettle is on and Elizabeth is settling a guest in, so come and let me update you."

"Update me on what?"

"There have been two more break-ins. One being Daphne and John Jones' place."

Christie stopped dead, hand over her mouth.

"She's fine, but she apparently disturbed the intruder. He got away though."

"I should go and see her."

"No. You should have a cup of coffee and sit for a while. That nice policeman said you'd want to help but he has to do his job first." Angus kept walking toward the kitchen, and Christie trotted after him.

"Can I talk to you?"

"Would you like some cake? Elizabeth made a delicious ginger-bread this morning." He collected cups from a cupboard.

"No, but thanks. I'm sure it is lovely." She perched on the edge of the table. "Can I help?"

"I saw that look. I'll have you know that Elizabeth works too hard and it is a pleasure to give her a small break. Now, where would you like to have this? Elizabeth will be back soon, if you want to wait."

"Actually, I need some advice, Angus. From you."

He shot her a glance. "What's wrong? Is it about the cottage?"

"Today has just been awful." Her phone rang. It was the third time Martin had called and once again, she rejected it.

"That was Martin, I saw his name come up. Why on earth not answer?" Angus stared at her in confusion, a cup in each hand. "Don't tell me he is what you want advice about?"

Not trusting herself to speak, she nodded, eyes wide.

"Let's go sit under the old tree then." Angus led the way.

"Tell me what to do." Close to tears, Christie pleaded. "I don't trust my judgement anymore."

Angus sipped the last of his tea. He'd listened to every word she'd said and wanted to pick up a phone and tell Martin to get himself down here right away. Overwhelming sympathy filled him, but she was wrong.

"It isn't my place to tell you what to do. And I believe you know the answers if you'd stop for a minute and think."

"I've been thinking. My head is ready to explode from it!"

"Well it won't explode so stop the melodrama and focus on what you really want. Instead of running away, why didn't you simply go and ask Martin why he took that woman to the yacht?"

"Because..." She looked down at her hands, playing with the empty coffee cup. "I mean, what if I do and he says I can't have *Jasmine Sea* anymore?"

"Why are you even thinking that way?" Angus put his hand over one of hers. "He loves you. Not in a destructive, controlling way like you might have experienced in the past, no, not at all like that. He loves you for who you are, even when you make mistakes."

Christie looked up. "Like leaving the window unlocked?"

"And not telling him."

"I didn't want to upset him."

Angus smiled as Christie's expression softened. "Okay, so we're as bad as each other." Her mobile beeped with a message. She read it aloud. *Randall and I will be at the lagoon at six. With dinner.*

"And where will you be at six, Christie Oliver?" Angus stood up and stretched.

Christie got to her feet and threw her arms around him. "Thank you."

"We all make mistakes. Wrong decisions that are sometimes based on a right motive. Talking, communication, that's the way to sort things out. Well, one of the ways," he grinned.

"Angus!"

"Come on. You might not have wanted gingerbread cake, but I do."

BREAKING

Derek stood on the balcony of the apartment, staring at the marina below. Yachts. Lots of them. Why the hell hadn't Christie told him she wanted one? He would have bought a decent boat with a captain and catering and all the comforts she deserved. He should have paid a bit more attention to her. But he'd always been generous. So many gifts and dinners. Trips away. Until it all fell apart with the death of her grandmother.

A key turned in the front door, which then swung open. Ingrid hurried in, closing and relocking the door behind herself.

"What the hell are you doing here?" Derek stalked inside.

Ingrid spun around in surprise, hand on heart. "God, you scared me! What are you doing here at this time of day?"

"None of your business. I'll have my key back." He held his hand out and Ingrid dropped it on his palm.

"Fine. But don't expect me to knock. Or even come over anymore." Ingrid went to the bar. "I just wanted somewhere to freshen up before coming to the office."

"And what's wrong with your place?"

"Have you heard from Rupert?" She poured herself a glass of brandy, then as an afterthought, one for Derek.

Martin packed up the plates and leftovers, until all that was left was the wine, the candle, and the rose on the table between them. He sat again and stared solemnly at Christie. "There are some things we need to talk about."

Heart sinking, Christie glanced away. For the past hour she'd pretended the rest of the day hadn't happened.

"Why do you assume the worst?"

Christie forced herself to meet Martin's eyes. He was unreadable. Not a wall, but a considered expression that gave nothing away. He took something out of the backpack and put it in the centre of the table. It was an origami boat.

"Unfold it." Martin suggested.

"Why did you... I mean, Ingrid?"

Martin sighed and sat back in his chair. "Okay, let's get this sorted. You do know I had no idea who she was?"

"Yes, but—"

"No, listen. Please. I had a client who, although annoying, was paying me a lot of money for a portrait. She got a phone call saying her mother, in England, was on her deathbed and begged me to set the portrait on the yacht. A last wish from her elderly parent."

Ingrid would have pleaded, probably with her hand on Martin's arm and her body leaning toward him. "Couldn't you have just super-imposed her onto a sketch without her actually being there?"

"How do you know I didn't?"

"Oh. Did you?"

"No. I only had the money on my mind, Christie. I didn't think it through."

Money? All those times...

Christie jumped to her feet.

"Sit down, sweetheart."

"All you've ever done is criticise me for having nice things. My car, jewellery. You've always thought those things matter to me and they don't, but now you're telling me they matter more to you than—"

"Than what? Than you?" His tone was mild. "Do you want to know why I wanted the money? Sit down."

Christie spun around and stormed away.

FOUR EMERALDS

She didn't make it off the jetty. Martin's arms swooped around her, stopping her in her tracks.

"Let me go!"

"Not going to happen. Now, you can come back to the table on your feet, or I can carry you."

The heat of his body radiated through Christie as he held her firmly against him, his mouth near her ear so she could hear him all too well. She held her body stiffly, resisting its annoying urge to sink into him.

"I recommend the first suggestion," he continued. "If I have to pick you up, I may just forget that we are out in public. We've had this discussion about your temper, and not very long ago."

"I'm really upset."

"Come on," he released her. "There's something you need to see." He walked away. Back to the table, where he stood waiting. Without his arms around her, a sudden chill made her shiver. The weather wasn't cold, but she was, inside. It took all of her self-control to go to him, but she did.

He motioned for her to sit, and pulled his own chair out. The origami boat was on the timber boards of the jetty and he scooped it up. When she sat, he offered it to her and this time, she took it.

"I don't know what screwed up ideas have gone through your head lately, but if they are about *Jasmine Sea* and Bethany or Ingrid, whatever her name is, then forget them. The facts are I wanted the money for a good reason, except things got to a point I wasn't prepared to deal with the devil any more. Unfold the boat, Christie. Please."

Her fingers struggled, still trembling with emotion. Then, as it opened, she realised what it was and her eyes flew to Martin's. "This is the boat registration."

"I know. Who is the registered owner?"

"Me." Her voice was tiny.

"And what is the date the ownership changed?"

She scanned the document. "This can't be right."

"Do you remember when we talked about your attraction to yachts in spite of your fear of water?"

"Before I went to Docklands Studios last time. You gave me *Jasmine Sea* all that time ago?" Her eyes were huge.

"I finally found something worth giving you."

"But you don't need to give me anything, Martin," she grabbed his hand, leaning forward. "Your love is everything. Not gifts or money or anything except you. And Randall."

He watched her for a while, then sighed deeply. "All I knew was that the most perfect girl in the world loved me. How could I compete with what you had? What you were used to? Why would you stay when your world was so far removed?"

Christie slipped out of her seat and dropped to her knees beside Martin. "This is my world." Her eyes glistened with tears. "My world, which I will fight for with every breath in my body."

Martin lifted her effortlessly to her feet as he rose to his. Christie noticed his hands were shaking a little.

What's wrong?

He looked so serious. "I know you're not ready. This is too soon, but I can't leave you wondering any longer. I can't wonder any longer." He released her hands.

Puzzled, Christie watched him fumble around in his pocket and pull out a small box. He suddenly grinned. "This had better not end up falling in the ocean. George will never forgive me."

Under the starlight, Martin sank onto one knee. Christie melted as he took hold of her left hand and gazed into her eyes. "I fell in love with you the moment I first saw you. You frustrated me and challenged me and utterly delighted me until I gave in and admitted to myself that you, Christabel Ryan Oliver, are the centre of my being. Will you marry me?"

Christie barely nodded.

"I think that was yes?" Martin opened the box. "Is it yes, Christie? Will you be my wife?"

Inside the box, on a bed of black velvet, was a diamond solitaire with four emeralds. They sparkled by the light of the lantern, perfect in a gold setting.

Randall padded over and sat beside Martin, leaning against him and looking at Christie with big, soulful eyes. "See," said Martin, "both of us are asking. We both need you."

Christie realised that she still hadn't spoken, and now tears were making everything misty. "Yes, Martin," she whispered. "Oh, yes, I will be your wife." For the second time in minutes, she dropped to her knees, this time to put her arms around Martin's neck. "I love you."

Randall buried himself between them.

For a long time Christie and Martin sat on the edge of the jetty, their feet dangling. They held hands, talking quietly about nothing at all. Anecdotes about other times and places. Little insights into each other's pasts. Every so often, they'd kiss. And laugh. As if barely believing it was on her finger, Christie kept sneaking looks at the ring.

"Do you like it?" Martin asked, his voice a bit worried. "If there's something else—"

"I love it! Did you say something about George? Did he make this?"

"He did."

"So beautiful." Christie watched the diamond and emeralds sparkle. "Four emeralds?"

"Your eyes are the same colour," he captured her hand. "One emerald represents the first time I saw you. The second reminds me of the first time I kissed you. The third is for tonight." He raised her fingers to his lips.

"And the fourth?"

"For the day we marry. And the diamond will be our children. You do want a family?"

She nodded, too overcome with emotion to speak.

Then yawned. Martin burst out laughing, stirring Randall, who looked up with an indignant groan.

"Sorry," she smiled, then yawned again. "I'm suddenly exhausted."

"I'll walk you home. It's been too long a day." Martin stood and offered Christie his hand. "Tonight you sleep and tomorrow we'll concern ourselves with any unresolved issues. We'll check up on Daphne in the morning, and see Trev. Okay?"

"Okay. I'm not going to argue."

Slinging the backpack onto his shoulders, Martin chuckled. "Let's get that in writing. In fact, I might prepare our wedding vows."

"What a terrible idea." She went to pick up the chairs but he got them first. "I can carry things."

"Grab the lantern. Light our way. Randall? You coming?"

Lantern aloft, Christie reached the beach and waited for Martin. Randall galloped past and threw himself onto the sand to roll. "You are very strange at times." Christie told him.

"Got your sandals?"

"In my bag. Which means I have a spare hand if you want me to take the chairs."

With a smile, he took her spare hand in his. "This is a better use for it." He leaned down and kissed her ever so gently. "I was afraid you wouldn't meet me tonight."

"What if I hadn't?"

"I'd have had to find someone else to give that ring to."

At Christie's outraged expression, Martin grinned and walked toward the river. She had no choice but to keep up with him because he had her hand tightly in his and wasn't letting go.

The fountain in front of Palmerston House drew Christie with its ever-changing colours. She'd said a long, passionate goodbye to Martin halfway down the driveway, insisting she was fine to get to the front door on her own. The day was catching up with him also, lining his face with exhaustion.

She trailed her fingers in the fountain, water trickling over her right hand. Her left she kept dry, watching the ring sparkle in the reflection of the lights. How perfect. One diamond, four emeralds, and each with a significance to Martin.

He wants children!

Together they would raise a beautiful family and have a home built on love.

"Are you planning on joining us for a nightcap, or are you going to stay out there?" Angus stood on the steps, the front door open behind him.

"Hello."

"Hello yourself. Everything okay?"

"Oh, Angus!" Almost bursting with joy, she ran up the steps and threw her arms around him.

"My goodness! Whatever is going on?"

She stepped back and held her hand out. "I kinda said yes."

Angus pulled her into his arms and squeezed her so much that she squealed. "Young Martin has excellent taste. And so do you."

"I'm the luckiest girl in the world. And guess what?"

"Are you going to jump up and down? You look as if you will."

"He wants to have children. Angus, I'm going to have a family one day!" A tear ran down her cheek and she wiped it away with a laugh. "Look at me, all emotional and silly."

"My dear child, you deserve to be happy. You deserve love and laughter and every good thing in life. I am so, so happy for you,"

Angus took her hand and linked it through his arm. "And now, we shall find Elizabeth, open a bottle of something special, and toast you both."

───────

Martin and Randall were both ready for bed as they climbed onto the deck. As Martin unlocked the door, Randall growled. The dog was rigid, staring in the direction of the studio with a low rumble resonating through him. Martin had never heard him growl. Ever.

"Stay put." Martin grabbed a flashlight from inside the door. Randall ran to the bottom of the steps, sniffing the air. "Go in the house."

Randall wagged the end of his tail, acknowledging the command but intent on whatever he sensed. Martin slid his hand under the dog's collar. "I need you safe." He had to tug at Randall to get him into the house, finally shutting him in.

Once he cleared the house, Martin turned the flashlight on, flicking it around. The studio was in darkness and there was nobody about. Perhaps Randall had picked up the scent of a stray dog or possum.

He stood at the door, feeling for his keys. But the lock was broken. Martin pushed the door open and turned on the lights. There was nowhere to hide in here and it was obvious that he was alone. He went from easel to easel. There was no damage.

In the middle of the studio, he stopped. Why? Someone had been here, broken in. But nothing was touched that he could see. Who was doing this?

Derek.

His gut told him that somehow that man was behind everything that had recently happened in River's End. Ingrid's deceptive behaviour reinforced it. Now, he had to prove it.

THE MORNING AFTER

C hristie wandered through the cottage not long after dawn, refreshed from a deep and happy sleep. Apart from the wet areas, now delayed thanks to the break-in, each room was almost complete. By the time Martha and Thomas returned, it would be ready for them to decide if they wanted it. If not, well, perhaps Rupert would be lucky and get it.

After locking the cottage, she checked the garage. Barry had wound a chain around the handles with a large padlock. All secure. Her foot crunched onto something. A shard of porcelain from the bath. Bits must have flown everywhere and it was surprising the person responsible hadn't been hurt. She wrinkled her brow, trying to remember something but was distracted by a cigarette butt a metre from the shard. None of the workmen smoked on site – Barry insisted on it – so whose was it? She squatted down. It reminded her of the butt she'd found smouldering at the end of the street.

She carefully picked it up in a tissue and buried it in a pocket. Most likely this was nothing, but finding two butts like this was odd. Very few locals smoked and she'd never once seen anyone toss a butt. It was worth showing to Trev.

Nauseous from downing almost the whole bottle of very fine whiskey, Rupert lay on the back seat of his car. He'd been there all night after stumbling around for hours in the dark. He thought he was parked somewhere between Martin's property and Willow Bay, up some hidden track, but his memory was fuzzy.

He had to get up; he needed to find a place for breakfast to settle his gut. With a bit of luck he'd find his way out of wherever he was and get to Warrnambool, which was more populated. If he could drive in a straight line.

Somehow he forced himself out of the car, leaning against it as the dizziness settled. Birds sang in the trees above, worsening his pounding headache. He slid into the driver's seat and closed his eyes, which didn't really help. An annoying alarm kept going off.

With a groan, he picked up his phone, which was somehow in the footwell of the passenger's side and ringing. "It's barely morning."

"We've got a problem."

"We always have problems," Rupert complained, closing his eyes again.

"Ingrid's vanished. I've been to her apartment, to the office, phoned her. Nothing."

"Well, she's not here—"

"Rupert. Shut up and listen. What did she do? Are the cops really involved?"

"Yes."

Derek swore. Rupert smiled to himself. Seemed that particular alliance was done.

"Where are you now?"

Rupert squinted at the trees. "Somewhere near River's End. But I'm not a suspect. Christie and Daphne still think I'm just this bumbling city guy looking for a sea change. I'm coming back to Melbourne later today."

"Not yet."

His mind was clearing now and he remembered Derek insisting any force was acceptable. "Boss, maybe you should come and do it. I'm not pushing the artist off a cliff."

"I don't want details. Just results."

Rupert stared out of the window, wondering when the money would get into his account.

"Are you still there?" Derek demanded.

"Boss. You know those voicemails from Ingrid, about doing over the studio?"

"Deleted of course."

"Nope. One of them is pretty incriminating about your part in this."

"What?"

"I'm not going to be working for you anymore. But I'd like a decent severance pay… if you get my drift, boss."

Derek screamed down the phone. "You get nothing! Nothing, you hear? There's no proof I've done anything other than send you to buy a property on my behalf. How you've conducted yourself is on you."

"So," Rupert continued as if Derek hadn't spoken. "I want double my salary and ten times my bonus in my account today."

"You'll get paid when you've split those two apart and I've got my cottage."

"Oh, and about splitting them. She's wearing his ring. He painted her with a lovely diamond and emerald engagement ring on… are you there?" Derek had hung up.

Never mind.

There was nothing keeping him here now. He lit a cigarette.

If he hadn't been in his office, Derek would have thrown his laptop against a wall. Rupert had to be lying. Christie would not marry Martin Blake. She was a sophisticated, educated woman with a successful career and a life in Melbourne. With him.

He dropped into his chair and put his head in his hands. This couldn't be happening.

"Sir?" There was a tap on the door.

"Get out, Lorraine. Hold my calls." He didn't lift his head.

"Sorry, sir, but the police are here."

Now, he looked up. Behind his secretary were two uniformed police officers. Were they here for Ingrid? Or him?

Damn her.

"See them in." Derek took a deep breath and got up. He waited to one side of his desk as they came in. One male, one female.

"Good morning, sir, I'm Senior Constable Mayer and this is Constable Todd." The female officer spoke and the male officer nodded.

"How can I help? Do you wish to sit?"

"Thank you, no. We are looking for your colleague, Ingrid Kauf—"

"So am I!" he interrupted, returning to his seat. "She owes me money and has disappeared in the middle of a straightforward job."

"What exactly was this job?"

"She wanted to look at some land on the coast with a view to us bidding on it. Last I know, she was there. I've tried to contact her for a couple of days, but no answer on her phone. I even went to her apartment this morning but no reply."

"When did you last speak with her?"

"I'm not sure. Maybe the day before yesterday? Look," he leaned forward in his seat, "she was missing her husband. He's in Germany or somewhere. She's probably just gone for a visit."

Senior Constable Mayer stared gravely at Derek. "Without informing you? Does she have friends, or other relatives we could speak to?"

"What's this about? She's not in trouble, is she?"

"Why would you suggest it?"

"You're worrying me. Ingrid was acting strange last time we spoke. Said she really wanted a piece of land or something and the people didn't want to sell it. She said she'd have to make them see things her way, but I thought she was joking."

Senior Constable Mayer put her notebook away and handed Derek a business card. "If you hear from her, or think of anything to help us locate her, please call."

The officers left, leaving the door open. Derek jumped up and closed, then locked it. He dialled Ingrid's number and again it went to her voicemail. He had no intention of leaving more messages. Between Ingrid and Rupert, they'd managed to stuff things up big time.

It didn't matter where she was. He'd done nothing wrong. And now he had only one priority. He tapped his intercom.

"Lorraine, arrange a hire car. I need it in one hour."

"Sorry, mate, gonna have to get forensics in but they'll take care with your paintings." Trev shook his head at the forced lock on the studio door. "Do you think he was disturbed before... well, any damage was done?"

"No. For some reason, whoever broke in either had no intention of vandalism, or changed their mind. God knows." Martin leaned against a wall. "There is one thing missing. A bottle of Chivas Regal Diamond Salute."

"Expensive?"

"Not cheap. But it was for Thomas, well, both of us. Nice on the deck after a long day."

"Most likely saw it there and swiped it. Guess in the scheme of things, losing a bottle of scotch is better than your paintings. What he did to Daphne is disgusting, all her nice things shattered. Keepsakes, things they'd collected on their honeymoon and for what?"

"And Christie's goods. Is this some kind of thrillseeker, Trev, or something more sinister?" Martin went to the painting of Christie and traced her face, smiling slightly as he remembered the feel of her warm skin against his.

Trev joined him. "What are you thinking?"

"Christie's ex is trouble. Last year he let himself into her place and gave her a scare. He's a narcissist through and through, charming one minute and close to violent the next."

"I had no idea. But what would he have to do with this?"

"Ingrid, or Bethany Fox, whatever her real name is, has a business partnership with him. They both want Christie's cottage. Scare campaign perhaps? Sending some message. Derek sent Christie a painting he'd bought after they broke up. It's one of my paintings. No note, no follow up contact so she doesn't even know if it now belongs to her, or is just part of some ploy to get her attention."

"I believe he'll get a visit this morning. Ingrid is proving elusive."

"Martin? Oh, no…" Christie ran in, hand to her mouth. "Your paintings?"

"It's okay, sweetheart. Nothing's damaged." Martin met her halfway and took her into his arms. "Just a bottle of scotch stolen and the lock broken." He felt her relax against him and loosened his hold.

She gazed up, worry in her eyes. "When?"

"Last night. Randall got all toey when we got back. Whoever did this was long gone, but I stayed down here just in case."

"You should have called me."

"No." His tone was firm and she nodded imperceptibly.

"Morning, Christie."

"Oh, sorry. Morning, Trev. Any idea who is doing all these dreadful things?"

Trev and Martin exchanged a glance. "Too soon. But the more fingerprints and other traces we get, the more chance of catching them. Anyway, hang around a bit if you can, Martin. I've got a couple of things to follow up." He nodded to them both, then hurried out.

Christie went to her portrait. She laughed softly. "When did you paint the engagement ring?"

"Around the time George and I designed it."

"Confident?"

"I asked the universe. Putting the ring where it belongs was simply the law of attraction."

Christie wound her arms up around his neck. "Oh, there's definitely a law of attraction here."

"Not even close. Ash, Martin asked me to marry him and I said yes."

"Oh, wait until I tell Ray! Congratulations, darling. Are you going to be alright? Can someone go to Auckland with you?"

"You know, if it was Derek, then he won't follow through. He's a coward and I will never let him near me again. Please, please don't worry. I'll talk to Martin and our local policeman and let them help."

With a sigh, Ash agreed. "Okay. But we're here if you need us. And we'll be there with an amazing wedding gift when you tell us!"

Christie was laughing as they said goodbye and disconnected the call. Her smile turned to a frown. What the hell was going on now?

Everything was against him, Rupert decided. He'd barely made it back to River's End before running out of fuel. Not far from the petrol station, he'd dug up a container and walked the short distance but couldn't pay. No cash on him, no money in his access account, and now his phone had died, meaning no way to transfer funds. He was directed to the only ATM in town and trudged his way there.

There was plenty of money in the linked account – thousands if Ingrid and Derek did as he told them – yet only an old-fashioned way of getting his hands on it. Hunger gnawed at his stomach and he was sure he was withdrawing from caffeine.

At the bank, he waited behind an old man who took forever to find his glasses, then his card. Eventually, he shuffled away from the ATM. Rupert glanced around. The street was quiet. He inserted his card, tapped in his number, and waited for a balance. Only the same amount as yesterday. Annoying as it was, this probably wasn't Ingrid or Derek's fault. Just banking delays. He transferred funds to his access account, withdrew some cash, and headed back to the petrol station.

Fuelled up, he left the car up the road from the corner cafe and pushed open the door, almost running straight into Daphne. "Sorry." He couldn't bring himself to look her in the eye.

"Oh, no, my fault. Not looking where I'm going." Daphne peered at him. "You look a little unwell, love. And you should get that cut checked."

"Um, just a shaving nick. Here, I'll get the door." He opened it quickly, hoping she'd leave, but she didn't move. Her long stare unsettled him and he shifted his weight between feet. "I'll bring Julie by next week and we'll have a look at those houses in the estate. She's getting a bit desperate before bubba arrives."

Daphne smiled and stepped through the doorway. "You do that, Rupert. John is always happy to show you around. Bye for now."

"Goodbye." Relieved, Rupert let the door close behind her. He needed to leave town.

TO CATCH A CRIMINAL

Outside the real estate agency, Christie spotted Daphne leaving the cafe on the opposite corner. Daphne glanced over her shoulder as she let a car go past, then hurried over, worry lining her normally happy face. Her eyes lit up when she saw Christie, and they managed a kiss to the cheek over the coffees.

"Something isn't right." Daphne announced, as Christie opened the door. She put the coffees on the counter. "I just ran into Rupert. I can't put my finger on it, but there's something about him that bothers me."

"It is odd that he's still here, instead of home with his wife. All he ever did was talk about Lucy and bubba." Christie said.

Daphne struggled for words. "Did you... Christie, what did you call his wife?"

"Lucy."

"He just called her Julie."

"Are you sure? It wasn't just noisy over there?"

"No, it was Julie. And that made me worry all the way back because I thought there was something wrong about it. What kind of man forgets the name of his own wife?"

Christie's phone beeped a message and she glanced at it. Ashley.

"And what's more, he has a cut on his cheek that doesn't look like any shaving nick I've seen!"

The shard.

A crunch underfoot near the garage. The cigarette butt near the bushes and the one at the end of the road. Rupert smoked.

"Where is he now?"

"At the cafe."

Both women rushed to the door. With coffee in one hand and a sandwich bag in the other, Rupert lumbered toward his car. A dark blue sedan.

"Oh, my," Daphne bristled. "Him!" She reached for the door handle but Christie stopped her.

"Phone Trev and tell him. I'll get the registration number and text it to him but you need to stay here! We can't alert him."

Without giving Daphne time to argue, Christie slipped through the door as Rupert got into the driver's seat. She darted across the road between cars. As soon as she was close enough, she took a photo of his car's plate and then pressed herself against a shop window.

She messaged the photo to Trev. Her own car was around the corner and following Rupert would end up in a chase, for he knew the Lotus. If he drove off before Trev got here, all she could do was point him in the right direction.

Her phone beeped again. Ashley. This time she read the message. *Ray saw Ingrid leave your apartment in a hurry yesterday. Derek was home. Thought you should know. Love from us both.*

A siren wailed in the distance. The sedan's engine roared and Rupert pulled straight out in front of another car. The driver slammed his brakes on, screeching to a halt just in time. Without pausing, the sedan flew along the road toward the mountains. Christie ran to check the driver of the other car, who although pale, waved that he was okay.

Trev's police car came into view. As he navigated around the stopped car, he wound his window down. "Everyone okay here?"

"Yes, but you need to get Rupert. He went straight ahead."

The police car accelerated. Daphne and John rushed out and,

drawn by the siren, townsfolk appeared on the street. Christie stepped back onto the pavement and the other car continued on its way.

Please catch him.

This had to stop now.

The minute he cleared the town, Trev let the patrol car loose. This was his community and nothing would stop him catching the sedan this time. He'd radioed dispatch, who were alerting the forensic team not to leave River's End just yet. All he had to do was find Rupert.

Five minutes on and Trev pulled over at the highest point of the road. He could see for kilometres ahead and there was not a car in view. Between town and here, Rupert had gone to ground, most likely down the side road Charlotte Dean had emerged from yesterday.

He doubled back, eyes flicking at each property he passed. There was an empty place with a fading For Sale sign on the front. On a few acres, the house was set back from the road and surrounded by dense bush. A glint at the far end of the driveway got his attention. He backed up and eased the car in.

Ever so slowly he followed the driveway, right past the house, to where a dark blue sedan was backed into bushes. Rupert sat in the front, eating. He dropped his food and pushed the door open. Trev leapt out. "Hold it."

"Officer. Just having breakfast." Rupert held his hands up, palms forward. "See, nothing in my hands."

"Step out slowly."

"Okay, okay. Man, can't get a few minutes peace for a quick bite." Rupert pulled himself out of the car with a grunt.

"Come to the front of the car."

"What'd I do? You can't arrest me for having breakfast."

"Bit late for breakfast. What are you doing parked here? This is private property."

"It's for sale. I've been looking for a house to buy for my wife—"

"Cut the bull. You've been identified as a person of interest in a break and enter."

"Me? No. I—"

"You've been drinking. I can smell it from here. Don't move." Trev looked in the car. "Interesting. That looks like a bottle of Chivas Regal. In fact, exactly like one stolen last night."

"I bought that."

"Where?"

"Local bottle shop."

Trev snorted. "Telling the truth will be better in the long run. Stay put, I'm going to do a breath test."

"Then what?"

"Then we'll be having a chat about what you are really doing in River's End."

Too excited to go back inside, Christie and Daphne waited on the pavement outside the real estate agency. John brought Daphne her coffee and squeezed her arm. "You've done well." With a kiss, he returned to work.

"I'm so sorry about what happened to you." Christie put an arm around Daphne's shoulders. "Trev will get him."

"Oh, lovely, it wasn't just me! All of your brand new appliances! And the poor family going into the estate. We've arranged for the mess to be cleared up but they are rather shocked. This doesn't happen in River's End!"

"No. And I'm so sorry." Christie dropped her arm. "I'm sure Derek is behind it."

"Well, shame on him! And thank goodness you escaped his clutches in time."

Christie grinned at Daphne's outrage. She played with her ring and, noticing the movement, Daphne looked at her hand. She squealed and Christie jumped. "What?"

Daphne grabbed Christie's hand. "Oh! He did it and you said yes!

Trev burst out of the interrogation room, leaving Jacqui to close and lock the door behind them both. He ignored Rupert's cry of "Hey, what about me?" He wanted a phone. And a detective, because this interview was over until someone with a higher pay grade took control. He couldn't make deals or start to know what to charge Rupert with.

"Jacqui, get onto Sarge and ask him to chase up some suits."

Jacqui sprinted to catch up with him. "Yes, sir."

"I'll need this joker taken to Warrnambool. Can't keep him here and it's almost time you head off."

"We can stay."

"No. Once you've done that, take Gareth and go. You've both been great." Trev stopped at his desk. "I mean it."

Jacqui nodded and got straight onto the phone.

Trev dialled his own phone. Melbourne was completely outside his area and his experience, but Senior Constable Katrina Mayer lived and breathed the city. They'd gone through academy at the same time but happily embraced their respective postings.

"Senior Constable Mayer," she answered.

"Trev Sibbritt."

"Thought the number was familiar. Do you have some news?"

"I have a confession. I can't do much until he's properly processed, but he's dropped himself right in it. And he's dropped your person of interest right in it with him."

"Ingrid Kauffman?"

"Got some voicemails from her I just listened to. In a nutshell, she directed him to break in to more properties, one being Martin Blake's studio. Said some pretty damning stuff about Christie Ryan and her cottage. Mentioned Derek Hobbs as being very unhappy if Rupert failed him."

"Well, that will help. Not that either of them are around. Forward them and I'll have a talk to the boss now and see what we can do to escalate the search for Ingrid. Is everything else okay?"

"Sure. You?"

"You know. Work. Kids. Never stops, but wouldn't swap it."

"Yeah. A good life."

After hanging up, Trev sat on the edge of his desk. He didn't even know she had kids now. He checked his watch. He wanted to get to Martin and Christie's party, have a drink with them to celebrate. With a bit of luck, he'd get Rupert out of here in time to shower and head over to Palmerston House.

Trev gave Rupert access to his mobile phone again. He stood behind him, making sure nothing was tampered with. "You'll get a chance to make phone calls soon."

"It isn't that."

"Then what? Photos of your family?"

Rupert glanced at Trev, annoyed. His imaginary family was one of the things that got him caught. The moment he'd said 'Julie' instead of 'Lucy', he'd realised his mistake. Daphne didn't seem to notice at the time, but Christie put it all together. Clever girl.

"I'm playing Candy Crush."

"Smart arse."

"I need to make sure I've got enough in the bank to post bail."

"What, won't Derek do it?"

"You know, under different circumstances I'd like to have a beer with you."

Trev grunted. "Not feeling it. You've caused a lot of distress to some fine people. Not exactly a good way to start a friendship."

"And I'll make up for it. Told you, I'll roll over on Ingrid. In a manner of speaking."

"And Derek?"

"He's just my boss. Nothing to do with this."

Trev shut up, more interested in watching Rupert log in to his bank account. The first account had a couple of hundred in it. Then, he switched to another account. His fingers flew up and down the

"What about Derek?" Martin had asked.

"He is a person of interest. At this stage, we want a nice chat."

"And when will that happen, Trev?"

"When he's located."

"Located?"

"Don't worry. His secretary finally told us he'd driven out to a new development west of the city. Sooner or later he'll front up at his office or apartment and will be making himself available to answer some interesting questions."

"You're sure he's not coming here?"

"I'm fairly sure Melbourne have it under control, Martin. All you need to worry about is dressing up nice for tonight so that your fiancée is proud of you."

Now, Martin smiled at the word fiancée. He glanced at his watch. With another hour and a half to the party, she'd be making herself beautiful about now.

61

SHIFT OF POWER

This wasn't possible. Yet, there he was, with a look of pure evil on the face she'd hoped never to see again. Christie's feet gripped the floor as though anchored.

Run.

Her heart wasn't beating, she was sure it wasn't, and there was no air in her lungs.

"The champagne won't bring itself in, Chris. Do you want me to get it?" Derek swung his feet over the side of the bed. He smiled. "My God, I've missed you so much."

A surge of outrage dominated the fear. "How dare you."

"What did you say?" Derek stood up.

"How dare you send me an anonymous note, knowing I would think it was from Martin! How dare you come on board my yacht and make yourself comfortable on my bed."

Derek burst into laughter. Hands clenched into tight balls, Christie glared at him. This wasn't the man she'd once loved.

He stopped laughing, but the sneer remained. "Your boat. Seriously, you don't even like the water so why would you buy a boat?"

"I didn't buy it."

"Ah. That's what he did to win your... affection. Outdo me. After

There was a way out of this mess. The yacht was drifting and with no anchor, anything could go wrong.

Back on deck, she realised just how far away from the mooring she'd come. Much longer and those rocks around the cliffs would have sunk the boat. Once the motor was started, she brought *Jasmine Sea* back to the channel. "Safe passage means keeping an even distance from each side. It's a good channel, deep and quite predictable in any weather, but also narrow. Stay in the middle."

His words spun in her head.

Deep.

Yes, of course the water was deep here. She scrambled to the seats and found a life jacket.

Derek wanted to kill Martin. She had no way of warning him or anyone else, thanks to the power cord that Derek must have cut when he boarded. He'd really thought of everything. Charm her with champagne, but just in case, make sure she had no way of calling for help.

"I'm not your little doormat anymore!" She screamed toward the beach. The wind whipped the words away but she didn't care. She had stood up to Derek. Stopped him from hurting her. Now, she had to protect the man she loved.

With a careful hand and using the last moments of dull light to guide her, Christie steered *Jasmine Sea* between the cliffs. The storm loomed from the south-west which would help her get to River's End. It was only around the headland, just a couple of nautical miles. This might be the hardest thing she'd ever do. But do it she would.

Martin had spoken of the laws of attraction. Christie visualised the jetty. It would be dark and the tide tricky, but she could get there and safely tie the yacht. Then, she'd get to his house, fly into his arms and he'd make everything alright again. A huge gust of wind slowed the yacht, the motor complaining. Christie cut it.

Now there was just the sound of the water and the occasional thunder. She was on the open sea. Above deep water.

Get to the jetty.

She forced her feet to move and her hands to follow the instructions she gave them. The boat creaked and groaned as she raised the sails and then the spinnaker filled and *Jasmine Sea* raced toward River's End.

Saturated, bleeding, and fuelled by an anger that made his head pound, Derek rowed to shore. In his whole life he had never been so humiliated. So hurt. As if his heart had been ripped out and thrown overboard alongside him. He'd gone to so much trouble to make things right and she'd lost her mind. He was going to find Martin Blake. And then he'd find Chris.

The dinghy stopped abruptly a couple of metres from shore and Derek swore as he clambered out into knee deep water. Everything hurt. He left the dinghy where it was and trudged onto dry sand. His shoes were on that yacht. Along with his fiancée.

"I love you, Chris." He did. She was his and one way or another, despite her confusion, she would find that out very soon.

Derek tried to make the flashlight on his phone work but not even one light would flicker. He threw it into the ocean. There was a flashlight keyring on his car keys, so he took those out and this time there was a small beam. He had to keep his thumb on the button, but after a couple of stumbles, got himself to the car park.

His foot still bled from sliding on the ice cubes, straight into the leg of the table, slicing between his toes. God, it hurt. He'd probably pick up some disease. Martin Blake would pay for that as well.

The trees enclosed him and he lost his bearings. His cut foot hit something metal and he almost screamed in pain, dropping to his knees. It was a crowbar. Pain forgotten, Derek got back up and worked out where he was. He smiled. First the artist.

WARNING OF DANGER

M artin stepped out of the shower to the sound of his phone. Almost tripping over Randall, who had a thing about laying across the bathroom doorway, he struggled to swipe the screen with damp fingers.

"Martin, Trev here."

"What's wrong?"

"Bit of an update. Is Christie with you?"

"No. She's at Palmerston House. Why?"

"Probably nothing. Our friend Rupert decided to spill his guts and it's pretty damning about Derek Hobbs."

Martin reached into the bathroom for a towel. "How."

"In a nutshell, Derek sent Rupert to buy the cottage. It was all on track as far as they were concerned, with Christie leading Rupert to believe she might consider it."

Martin put the phone on speaker and dropped it onto the bed as he dried himself. "Okay. If he says so."

"Anyway, with Ingrid butting in and starting her chain of events, Derek got hot under the collar and told Rupert he wanted results. At any price. Your name came up quite a bit and so did hers."

"Did he threaten Christie?" Tossing the towel into a washing basket with more force than he needed, Martin's voice hardened. "I'm heading down there now."

"The threats were more against you, mate. Look, we don't know where he is. No sign of him at his office or apartment and now it turns out he booked a hire car a few hours ago."

"So, he's heading here?"

"Probably not. More than likely he's gone to meet up with Ingrid and its all bluff and bravado. But keep an eye out, okay?"

"Are you coming along tonight?"

"Expect to. At this rate, I might stay in kit."

"I'll see you shortly." Martin hung up and dialled Christie, taking the phone off speaker. It went straight to voicemail and he grimaced. "Sweetheart, I'm leaving in five minutes, but do me a favour and stay close to Angus. Give Trev a ring if anything odd happens, okay? See you soon."

So much for charging her phone.

We'll talk about that.

Calling the landline at Palmerston House would only slow him now, and he'd be there in a few moments anyway. He finished dressing and threw on some shoes.

Randall followed him through the house as Martin collected his wallet and keys. "Better you stay here." He patted Randall's head at the door. "No point us both getting wet on the way home."

The air was still hot and sticky but a strong breeze warned of the imminent change ahead. Martin slid the door closed. Lightning forked into the sea out along the horizon and he turned to watch heavy clouds scuttle across the darkening sky. A long, low rumble of thunder followed. At least Christie was safe with their friends.

———

Palmerston House was a picture as Martin drove Thomas' old four wheel drive along the driveway. The first sprinkle of rain had begun as he'd left his house, so he'd gone back for the car keys and thankfully it started first time. It occurred to him that having something other than his motorcycle would be a likely addition in the future. Christie's Lotus was all very well for her needs, but once they had a family, they'd need a second car.

Soon, Thomas and Martha would be home, and Christie was only going to be away for a fortnight. He'd use the time to finish his painting and make a plan for them both. Then they could work out the details and decide a date to marry. For the first time in his life, Martin had purpose beyond his art.

No more days and nights that drifted into weeks and months, with him rarely leaving the property, except to shop or give George a chance to attend his council meetings. Randall was an amazing companion, but now there was more. Light and life, love and passion filling him with a yearning to begin.

He drove around the fountain and parked facing back to the road. The rain stopped. As he got out, Angus came through the open front door. By the time Martin reached the steps, Angus was at the bottom, worry in his eyes.

"You look concerned." Martin shook his hand.

"It's just that…" Angus glanced down the driveway. "We thought Christie must be with you."

"Angus? Is she not here?"

"No."

Martin turned to leave, but Angus put a hand on his arm. "Come inside. We need to show you something." Angus dropped his hand and went back up the steps.

Martin followed. "When did she leave?"

"We've not seen her since this morning."

Elizabeth was just inside the door, her smile dropping when only Angus and Martin came in. "Oh. She's not with you."

"No. I've got to find her."

"Martin, what about the note though?" Elizabeth hurried to the roses and extracted the note. "I wouldn't pry, but Christie dropped by earlier and left these. We didn't see her, just heard the car, but we got concerned with the storm coming and tried to call her."

"She let her battery go flat." Martin forced the words out.

Where is she?

"The note, dear. To meet you on the yacht."

"I didn't send a note. Or roses."

"It says 'meet you on the boat at five p.m.' but if you didn't send it, then who did?"

expression gave away his thoughts and Martin stalked across to the dinghy he'd retrieved. "Whose blood is it then?"

Trev turned the light on the dinghy. "No way of knowing. Maybe she cut herself. Maybe it's his. But speculating isn't finding her so I'd suggest we get going."

Both men jogged up the slope to the carpark, the wind at their backs.

"What the hell?" Trev spotted a trail of blood leading into the bushland. Just a few drops here and there, and washing away as the rain intensified, but a trail nonetheless.

"Whoa. Stop. Look there." Trev focused the flashlight on a dark spot in the bushes.

"What is it?"

"Balaclava. As in, the one used by Rupert. Whoever the blood belongs to, they've stumbled on Rupert's stash."

"Stash?"

"He threw away his balaclava. And a crowbar."

Martin was quiet. Trev glanced at him. "What?"

"The wind is coming from the south-west. Christie knows to go with the wind. We need to leave." Galvanised, Martin rushed to Thomas' car. The motor turned, groaned, and spluttered.

"You know, I have these things called siren and lights. Wanna lift?" Trev grinned as Martin leapt out again.

The patrol car only got to end of the track before pulling over when a second unit turned in. Trev got out to speak with Jacqui and Gareth.

Flashing lights, rain, night time. The terror of some incomprehensible event. Martin pressed his fingers against his temple. He barely remembered the night his parents and grandmother died. Such a little boy, secure in a booster seat. Uniformed police milled around, that he recalled. Concerned voices.

Panic.

Thomas arriving. His beloved, strong grandfather weeping at a funeral for three.

Christie promised she'd never leave him. Outside the cottage, under starlight, she'd taken his hands and assured him she would always return if she needed to work. She understood his childhood loss. Two of a kind, yet so different in the way they managed the pain. And somehow, they'd found each other.

Trev slid back behind the wheel. "We're going." He glanced at Martin as he started the motor. "You right?"

"We need to get to the jetty."

"Yup. Going now." He eased the car onto the main road and put the siren on. "Those two will dig around in the bush and keep an eye out, in case she comes back in."

"What if he has her?"

"Coast Guard isn't far away."

"We need more people looking."

"More are coming. What you need to do is stay calm, and as your friend, I know that's hard. Focus on what we know. There's a KALOF out on the car that Derek Hobbs hired."

"A what?"

"Shorthand for don't miss it going past."

"I need to update Angus."

"Call him."

Trev's radio crackled. The conversation made little sense to Martin, but a few words from dispatch and Trev accelerated. "There's been a sighting of a car that might be his."

"Where?"

"Heading to the cottage."

"Drop me near the jetty."

"Best I can do is the bridge, mate. Take my flashlight and follow the river. Phone me as soon as you get there. Right?"

Martin nodded, dialling Palmerston House. In a few minutes he'd be on his feet and one way or another, he'd find his girl.

beach, where the stone steps led to the graveyard. There was a person running toward her. Not running. Hobbling.

Hand still on the rope, horror swept through Christie as Derek drew closer. He waved and yelled. There was no way to get off the boat and then the jetty. Terror froze her in place.

Randall barked. It wasn't just about her any longer. She undid the rope with a quick tug. Before she could change her mind, Christie threw herself to the wheel and wrenched it away from the jetty.

Derek was there. He screamed at her, over and over. "Stop. You have to stop."

He was going to kill her. And Martin. She realised she'd started the engine and just as Derek got close enough to grab the side of the yacht, she widened the distance.

INTO THE STORM

A ngus hung up the phone and turned frantic eyes to Elizabeth. The others – Daphne and John, Sylvia, and Barry – huddled around, wanting to know what Martin said.

As each had arrived, Elizabeth had recounted the little that they knew. Christie was missing, presumed lured to *Jasmine Sea* by her ex-fiancé. Emotions from anger to fear filled the small group. Angus paced the floor, inconsolable until the phone rang.

"Martin is going to the jetty. The hope is Christie is alone on the yacht and heading for the beach."

"How does he know that?" Daphne gripped John's hand.

"Educated guess. He is being dropped at the bridge in a moment or two."

"Where is Trev?" Barry demanded.

"Apparently the car Derek Hobbs hired was seen going toward Christie's cottage."

"I'll go." Barry strode toward the front door.

"Please wait. Martin might need us. The police are quite capable of going there without any of us getting in the way and we should stay here. We should gather some blankets and towels. And... well, we

ONE DOWN

Thankful to have escaped from Martin Blake, Derek wanted to get to his car and leave. Whatever happened to Chris was out of his control. She'd chosen to sail into a storm and it wasn't his fault.

Pain shot through his foot with every step. Being flattened to the ground had added to the damage and there was blood squishing inside his shoe. He cursed his moment of weakness in telling the artist there was a hole in the boat. But nobody could prove he put it there.

At the bottom of the stone steps he stopped to try to see what was happening out in the water, but the yacht was invisible. The hero had jumped in to save her. Good luck with that. They might both go down in the shipwreck.

Reminiscent of that painting, *Sole Survivor*. Not once had Chris thanked him for his generosity. Sending it to her as a gift was his way of saying sorry for any misunderstandings. No words of appreciation from her. Just silence.

He wished he'd never started this. Nobody could ever say he hadn't tried. Loving someone as much as he loved Chris meant sacrifices. Their love would live forever, even if she didn't. He noticed an engraving on the smooth cliff face. A love heart with the initial T at the top, and M at the bottom. Another time and he'd do a replica. D loves C. Pity she'd never see it.

Sick of being wet through, Derek climbed the steps. He stopped a few times to look out over the ocean. The rain fell in sheets and only once did he think he'd caught a glimpse of the boat. By now it would be taking in lots of water and Christie must surely know.

He dropped his head.

Goodbye, Chris.

Finally at the top, he realised too late that his car was blocked by two police cars. Lights flashing, they barred his escape. Three police officers huddled at the back of his car. As one, they saw him.

"Not a fan of storms." Something caught Charlotte's attention through the picture windows. "What's that light? In the sky?"

George got to his feet and followed her to the front of the foyer. "I can't be sure."

"What is it, George?" Elizabeth followed as George opened the front door and went outside. From the top of the steps, in the direction of the beach, a bright light hung in the sky.

"That is a flare from *Jasmine Sea*." George declared.

"Angus, Barry, everyone! There's a flare. We need to go." Elizabeth ran back inside.

Each powerful stroke of his arms, every kick of his legs, Martin mentally recited one phrase.

Christie Blake. Christie Blake.

Imagine what will be and see it come true.

She was alive and he would find her. Their lives were mapped out. A short engagement. The most romantic wedding imaginable. Children. Happiness. More dogs. He would paint and she would follow whatever dreams she might find. He visualised their lives.

The rain was gone and the strong wind more of a breeze. He calculated he was halfway to *Jasmine Sea*, assuming she hadn't drifted too far. He should have got more information from Derek. What part of the hull was holed? The easiest place would be in the engine room and that gave Martin some hope. If the hatch stayed secure, the yacht wouldn't sink. Not for many hours. The risk was more around Christie losing control of the steering.

Christie Blake.

He saw her as his wife. How he loved her. So beautiful and so very generous. Her warm heart and gorgeous smile brought a light and happiness to his world. Everyone in the whole town adored her. She'd even won over Sylvia despite their early issues around Belinda. Randall worshipped Christie and would probably live with her over Martin any day. Fortunately, Randall wouldn't have to choose because once she was back in his arms, Martin was never letting go again.

The black night suddenly lit up and Martin thought it was a close lightning strike. But the light stayed bright and he stopped swimming to paddle upright. It was a flare and now he saw *Jasmine Sea.*

Relief warmed him. Taking a moment to let his muscles rest, he watched the yacht. It was leaning heavily to starboard now.

"Christie! I'm coming!" He called with all of his power. He couldn't see her but she would be at the highest point of the deck. Once he got to her, he'd keep them afloat until the Coast Guard arrived. Martin kicked forward and resumed his rhythmic stroke.

Christie Blake. Christie Blake.

After a moment she glanced up. "Okay, turn him. He's actually conscious but exhausted. Hey dude, are you okay?" Her voice softened as she lowered her face to look in Randall's eyes. There was the barest flicker of a wag from his tail.

"You're a doctor?" Trev adjusted Randall as instructed.

"Psychiatrist. I should have been a vet."

"No. I didn't mean that. It's great."

"Oh, Randall." George leaned down to touch Randall's head. "No, Martin will be inconsolable."

"He's okay, George."

"But, Trevor, he looks…"

Randall moaned and tried to sit up. "Steady on." Charlotte supported his head. "Can we get him onto a blanket and start drying him? And some water for him."

Trev lifted Randell with a glance out to sea. Where was Christie?

74

WHEN ALL IS LOST

The water was shallower now, Martin felt the difference below them. Christie's hands were locked together behind his neck and she gave feeble kicks to help. He wanted to tell her to relax, but his own muscles had little left in them.

Her eyes were afraid and exhausted and something else he couldn't work out. What she had been through he couldn't guess at. All he knew was he'd found her and she was alive. Just very, very quiet.

I found you.

If his hands were free he would have held her to him.

"I'm so sorry," she whispered.

"You've done nothing wrong. Save your strength."

"Randall."

"The only one of us warm and dry."

"He was on board."

Gut wrenching fear tore at Martin. "On board?"

"I got the collar on him. He was swimming to shore. I'm sorry."

"Can you swim again?"

Christie answered by unclasping her fingers and sliding into the water. Martin stayed at her side, swimming stroke for stroke. He had to get Christie to the beach, then he had to find his dog.

A blinding light flashed on him. "Christie, wait." There was a boat. "Here! We're over here!" He raised his arms.

"Got you! Hang on, we're coming." Barry's voice boomed across the water.

"Christie, it's okay." Martin reached for her, pulling her to him again. She didn't seem to understand. "Nearly over. I'll find Randall."

A moment later the inflatable closed in. "Thank God!" Barry cried. "Christie, let's get you in."

Martin steered Christie to Barry. "Lift your arms." She did so, his arm around her until Barry took over, pulling her into the boat, where she curled up on the floor.

Barry leaned back over. "Now you, mate."

"Randall."

"At the beach. Look, I think… Martin, wait, we can row you back."

Martin swam as fast as he'd ever swum. From the light of Barry's flashlight he'd worked out where he was. They'd drifted down the beach quite a bit and he knew he'd get there before the inflatable. He couldn't save Christie just to lose his dog. Adrenalin surged through him and he powered through the waves.

Close enough to put his feet down, he waded, his legs shaking. There was a group of people near the jetty. Lights. A table. Was someone having a picnic? His mind couldn't comprehend what he saw.

"Look! It's Martin!"

He thought that was Elizabeth. Why would she be here? He staggered into the shallows, barely able to stay upright. His vision cleared and he recognised Angus, Daphne, John. Others were too far away. A woman sat on a blanket with… it was Randall. Flat on his side.

Martin fell to his knees on the tideline with a heart wrenching cry, "RAN-DALL!" Tears blinded him. He'd failed his dog. Oh God, Thomas. The man who'd given him Randall as a puppy, loved him every bit as much as he did. He'd failed them both.

Something hit him hard and he crashed onto the sand. A wet tongue licked his face and then Randall flopped at his side.

"He's okay, Martin. Just exhausted. Oh, I'm so sorry you thought he might be gone, my boy." George stumbled over the sand to them. In disbelief, Martin put his arms around Randall. He was real and very alive.

George helped Martin to his feet. Martin lifted his dog and carried him back to the blanket. He gently lowered him and then his legs gave out and he sat down with a thud. Randall was happy to lay down, this time with his head in Martin's lap.

"Martin, where is she?" Angus cried in distress.

"In the boat. Look, there it is."

Barry's boys, John, and Angus met the inflatable. Martin got to his feet and his legs immediately gave way again.

Angus strode into the shallows and scooped Christie into his arms. Her head rolled to one side, her arms and legs hanging. Trev helped him to another blanket near Martin.

"Christie. Christie, it's over, sweetheart." He reached for her hand. She was so white, so lifeless. Randall whined and crawled to her. He licked her face and suddenly, her eyes blinked. Tears streamed down Martin's face as he squeezed her hand and she faintly returned the pressure. He gave in to the exhaustion and lay on his side, holding her hand, Randall between them.

75

TWO DOWN

O utside Melbourne International Airport, Ingrid glanced at the night sky. A storm was coming. It better not delay the flight. Australia might be her birthplace, but her time here was over, thanks to Derek Hobbs.

She wheeled her trolley of suitcases through the sliding doors and headed to business class check-in. Another day and she'd be back in London, then on a train to Switzerland. A week in the Alps and she would decide whether to reconcile with Leon, or look further afield. Pity really, Derek had been fun but his obsession with his ex was boring.

What did annoy her was the lost opportunity. Had her hands not been tied, she might have made quite a bit of money, not to mention being a thorn in Bryce Montgomery's side. Employing Rupert was a dreadful idea, and when he tried to blackmail her, she almost let him. Once she gave it proper consideration, it was obvious that he was bluffing. With a bit of luck he would rot in some prison.

The line moved and she pushed her trolley to the desk. "I'm on flight—"

"Ingrid Kauffman?"

Ingrid spun around. Two Australian Federal Police stood behind her. She forced a fake smile. "Officers? How can I help?"

"We'd like you to accompany us to an interview room."

"Really? I am a dual citizen and racing home to see my dying mother. You can talk to me when I return."

"We've been advised that your mother regrettably passed away several years ago. Would you prefer to accompany us in a peaceful manner, or should we read your rights and handcuff you here?"

Her eyes darted around. People stared. The police stared. She was trapped. God, what had Derek done! "I'll come with you."

"Excellent decision."

Christie locked the cottage and checked it twice, making Martin laugh. "Would you like me to give the key back to Barry?" Barry had dropped his set around to Palmerston House once word got out that Christie's were missing. "He's given the boys the day off and taken one himself. He mentioned something about returning some baskets to Sylvia."

"Thanks. What will I do about the Lotus though?"

"Drive it?" Trev came around the corner of the cottage. "Nice to see you looking so... dry." He shook Martin's hand and kissed Christie's cheek. "Feeling a bit better today?"

"Everything hurts, but yes. But how do I drive the Lotus without keys?"

"Cleared them from evidence. Here." Trev took her car and cottage keys from a pocket. "Just one of many problems looming ahead for one Derek Hobbs."

"Thank you so much" Christie took the keys. "Trev, was there anything... else on him?" Her voice faltered and she unconsciously touched her ring finger.

"It wouldn't feel right for me to do this, so here, Martin." Trev took Christie's ring out of a different pocket and handed it to Martin.

Christie let out a small sob and tears flooded her eyes. Martin looked skyward. "Christie, no more crying! Now, this is your last chance to change your mind. Still want to marry me?"

She nodded, blinking rapidly to clear the tears, but one fell onto Martin's hand as he took hers. He slipped the ring on and kissed her hand. Then he found a handkerchief and dabbed her eyes.

"Thanks, mate." He nodded to Trev, who sported a big grin.

"All good. I'll need you both for statements today. Sorry, but the sooner we do it, the faster I can escalate charges. Say, an hour from now?" He waved and headed back to his car.

"I don't want to leave." Christie whispered, staring at her ring.

"The cottage?"

"River's End."

"We'll be here," Martin said. "Randall and I, we will be here. And you'll come home and we'll get married. So, there it is."

You're right.

Christie smiled. "Yes, there it is."

78

THE TOUCHES OF A HOME

E xcitement bubbled up in Christie as the Lotus hugged the final curve before home. The ocean stretched out forever, sparkling and inviting under the early autumn sky. Two weeks made a noticeable difference at this time of year, particularly the deciduous trees with their blaze of yellow, red, and orange.

A quick phone call to Martin when she cleared the airport had her curious. "Go to the cottage first. There's a surprise for you." It was too far past lunch for a picnic and they were expected at Palmerston House tonight for the delayed engagement party.

She turned into her street, singing along to the radio as she navigated the familiar potholes and railway track. Instead of going up the driveway, she parked on the grass verge. Her bags could come in later. There was no sign of Martin, but then again, last time she'd returned from a job, he and Randall were already inside the cottage.

In delight, she halted at the gate. Gone was her dreadful attempt at drawing a door and in its place was the real one. Two new steps led to a security screen door. The smell of freshly mown grass took her attention. Not only mown, but there was a new path to the front door. Whatever had Martin been up to? She went around the back.

At the porch she stopped, hand over her mouth. There was a love seat and a hanging basket of jasmine. The tendrils touched her as she unlocked the door and she inhaled their scent with a smile. "Martin? Randall?" She called, stepping in.

The kitchen was finished. New sink, appliances, and re-varnished floorboards. The old kitchen table still dominated the room, but it was now lacquered a rich mahogany.

Room by room, Christie inspected the cottage, gasping at the changes. The curtains were hung, flooring all done, laundry and bathroom beautiful with brand new fittings and appliances. Like a new house!

Like a home.

Vases of flowers adorned the bedrooms and lounge room, and Martin's painting of her hung above the fireplace. There was still plenty to do, but someone had put a lot of love and effort into this.

The end of the hallway was transformed. Christie walked right into a gorgeous little entry. Thomas' paintings adorned two walls, and there was a narrow table, clearly crafted by Martin. Beneath it, more of Thomas' paintings were lined up.

She opened the front door and the screen door, and stood on the top step smiling at the garden. What a difference from the overgrown, sad old building she'd inherited.

The sound of a car broke the silence. She recognised the old four wheel drive and wondered why Martin would come in that instead of his motorcycle.

It turned into the driveway and stopped. Christie squealed as Thomas climbed out of the back seat and opened the front door for Martha.

"I can't believe it!" Christie jumped up and down, and then ran toward the driveway, just as Martin appeared from around the back of the car. Like a bullet, Randall raced past everyone, straight to Christie, and she leaned down to hug him. He whimpered and wiggled in joy, licking her face as she told him how much she'd missed him.

"Does this happen often?" Thomas asked Martin. Christie looked up at them, Martha with her arms open, Thomas shaking his head, and Martin grinning. "All the time." Martin replied. "She has her priorities right."

As much as she wanted to fly into his arms, it was Martha she went to first, once she'd extricated herself from doggie kisses.

"My darling!" Martha embraced Christie and kissed her cheek. "You beautiful child! I have missed you so very, very much."

"Stop hogging her." Thomas complained. "What about me, young lady?"

"Oh, Thomas, I can't believe you're both back!" Christie dived at him and he laughed as he enfolded her in a bear hug, almost swinging her off her feet. Randall ran around them both.

"See, Martha. This is what you'll have to get used to. Randall really only cares about them." Martin put an arm around Martha's shoulders.

"So I see," she said. "Shall we go?"

"Don't you dare!" Christie slid away from Thomas and turned to Martin. "Hi."

"Hi." He held out a hand and she accepted the invitation. He kissed her and tiny sparks of electricity lit up her nervous system. When she opened her eyes, it was to look straight into his own dark pools so often unreadable. Not now. There was promise and desire in their depths.

"My God." Thomas stared at the open front door. "What have you done?"

"I remember the front door." Martha put her hand on Thomas' arm. "Oh. I remember everything, Tom."

"Granddad, I should have warned you."

"It is just a door." Strain coloured Thomas' voice.

"Okay, before this gets out of hand, I insist you step through my front door, Thomas!" Christie took his hand and tugged. He stayed where he was. "Hey, trust me," she pleaded.

Something about her tone of voice got his attention and he let her lead him to the steps. She released his hand and stood back with a smile. "It's something good, I think."

As though to humour Christie, Thomas stepped into the entry way. There was a moment of silence, then "Martha! Martha come quickly."

Martha almost broke into a sprint to reach him and Christie grabbed her arm to steady her up the steps, Martin right behind.

"What is it, dear? Oh, my."

Thomas had his arm over Martha's shoulders and she had hers around his waist. They surveyed the paintings on the walls and on the table. Martha found him a tissue and he brushed away tears.

"Granddad?"

"You're not in trouble. So it isn't granddad." Thomas emerged with a look of wonder. "Someone had better explain this."

"Nobody knows for sure, but it seems your father sealed the paintings in. When Barry took the cupboard out, there they were." Christie said.

"And brushes and paints, Thomas." Martin added.

Martha followed Thomas back onto the lawn, holding tightly onto his arm. "What a day."

"And this probably isn't the best time, but, well I want to offer you both the cottage. As a gift from me." Christie rushed the words. "It's almost completely renovated with new appliances and—"

"Darling," Martha interrupted. "This is your home."

"Yes. But if you would live here… if you feel you could live here, then nothing would make me happier than to gift it to you both."

"It's not as though she'll be living here for long." Martin threw in and Christie turned a startled look at him. "Probably not even for another day."

"I won't? Okay. Yes, Martin."

"Yes, Martin? What have you been doing to this poor child?" Thomas asked, winking at Martha. "Martha and I will talk about it."

With a huge smile, Christie hugged him, and then Martha. "Go inside and see!" She insisted.

Alone with Martin, she stole a glance at him. "You want me to move in with you?"

"Randall does."

"Oh. Randall does. Well, I'd better make him happy then."

Martin reached for Christie.

79

WHERE TRUE LOVE LIVES

M usic and laughter filled Palmerston House. The fountain bubbled its ever-changing coloured water and fairy lights decorated the long verandah. Inside, people danced and talked, toasted each other, and swapped stories about the night of the storm. With Thomas and Martha home, there was extra joy and celebration.

"Thank you so much, Elizabeth!" Christie emerged from the kitchen with a tray of bite-sized quiches. "Palmerston House looks magnificent and you also look stunning." She kissed Elizabeth on the cheek.

"Me? Oh, thank you. You are the guest of honour, by the way, and should let me take that around."

"Not a chance. Anyway, I think someone is going to ask you to dance." Christie grinned as Angus approached. "Aren't you, Angus?"

"What was the question?"

"Elizabeth wants to dance."

"Christie! I did not say that—"

"What a good idea. Shall we?" Angus offered his arm. Elizabeth gave Christie a perturbed look, but took his arm, and they ventured onto the dance floor.

BOOKS BY PHILLIPA NEFRI CLARK

River's End Mystery Romances

The Stationmaster's Cottage

Jasmine Sea

The Secrets of Palmerston House

The Christmas Key

Taming the Wind

Martha

Notes from the Cottage

The Charlotte Dean Mysteries

Deadly Start

Deadly Falls

Deadly Secrets

Deadly Past

The Giving Tree

Daphne Jones Mysteries

Till Daph Do Us Part

The Shadow of Daph (coming soon)

Tales of Life and Daph (coming soon)

Doctor Grok's Peculiar Shop Fantasy Shorts

Colony

Table for Two

Wishing Well

Sculpture

Or get the entire collection in one:

Doctor Grok's Peculiar Shop Short Story Collection

Last Known Contact

Simple Words for Troubled Times

Prefer Audiobooks?

The Stationmaster's Cottage

Jasmine Sea

The Secrets of Palmerston House

Simple Words for Troubled Times

RECOMMENDED READING ORDER

The River's End series includes four main books (The Stationmaster's Cottage, Jasmine Sea, The Secrets of Palmerston House, The Christmas Key), plus three short books.

Taming the Wind can be read anytime. Before or after the others will still make sense.

Martha is best read after Cottage and some readers enjoyed it more after reading The Christmas Key.

Notes from the Cottage contains spoilers and should be read after The Stationmaster's Cottage. It is a behind-the-scenes look at the writing of TSC rather than a new fiction book.

There are also two spin-off series to enjoy.

The Charlotte Dean Mysteries begin shortly after The Secrets of Palmerston House. They are best read in their series order.

The Daphne Jones Mysteries are set after The Christmas Key. These also are best read in series order.

Last Known Contact is a stand alone crime suspense, unrelated to the other series.

Simple Words for Troubled Times is a non-fiction short book to offer comfort and happiness.

Future books include a fantasy trilogy, a new crime suspense, and more in the various series.

Thank you for reading one of my stories - I am so thrilled you took a chance on me and hope you enjoyed your time in my world.

Printed in Great Britain
by Amazon

All about the ket

low in carbohydrates and rich in fats and proteins

Josh Motley

INTRODUCTION..5
WHAT IS THE KETOGENIC DIET 7
Ketosis...7
Are we in ketosis? the first symptoms 8
Various low carb diets..8
KETO...11
Ketogenic diet: how to reach ketosis..11
Ketogenic diet: what to eat..12
What to eat in quantity 12
You can eat but in limited quantities and recommended by your doctor: ...13
What not to eat 13
A ketogenic diet is usually composed as follows..........................14
Contraindications of keto diet...15
Ketogenic diet: Who can do it? 16
The ketogenic diet cannot be recommended for those who 16
POST-DIET 18
Why it didn't work 18
Ketogenic diet: contraindications...19
KETO CRESCENT DOGS 21
REAL TEXAS CHILI 21
FRIED CABBAGE WITH CRISPY BACON 21
BEEF FA-KETO DISH 22
EASY KETO SWEDISH MEATBALLS 22
KETO BLT WITH OOPSIE BREAD 23
PULLED PORK WITH MANGO SAUCE 23
CAULIFLOWER CASSEROLE TWICE BAKED KETO.....................24
KETO TUNA SALAD WITH HARD-BOILED EGGS 24
STEAMED MUSSELS WITH PIRI PIRI 24
CASHEWS AND BROCCOLI...25
LOW-CARB KETCHUP STEAK WITH BLUE CHEESE ONION CREAM SAUCE 25
KETO DINNER...27
Lemon and Sage Creamed Chicken 27
Fried salmon with asparagus 27
Easy Stuffed Peppers..28
Keto Pizza Meatballs and Mushrooms 28
Salmon with Pistachio Pesto...29
Deconstructed Pork Eggs 30
Best Keto Brownies 30
Boneless pork chop and zucchini spears.......................................31
Meatloaf and red pepper glaze on the sides 32
Wonton Soup 32
Chicken Saltimbocca 33
Chicken Jambalaya Sausage and Andouille..................................33
Keto Asian Noodle Bowl..34
Keto Scramble with Sausage..34
The Keto Site 35

Snak Keto 37
    Low carb snacks: 6 low carb snacks 37
    Fresh fruit in season 38
    Centrifuged drinks 38
    Dried Fruits 38
    Yogurt 38
    Vegetables 38
    Low-carb grains 39
21 Days Plan 41
    WHAT IS THE KETOGENIC DIET AND HOW DOES IT MAKE YOU LOSE WEIGHT IN 10
    TO 21 DAYS 41
    THE KETOGENIC DIET: A SCIENTIFIC APPROACH 41
    FOR WHOM THE KETOGENIC DIET IS INDICATED 42
    CONTRA-INDICATIONS OF KETOGENICS 43
    EVIDENCE SUPPORTING THE KETOGENIC DIET 43
    KETOGENIC DIET WHAT TO EAT 44
    FOODS TO AVOID IN ORDER TO INDUCE KETOSIS 45
    WEEKLY SCHEME KETOGENIC DIET (DIMA METHOD) 45
    PROGRESSIVE REINTEGRATION DIET (POST-CYCLE) 46
    THE PHASES OF THE KETOGENIC DIET 47
    FREQUENTLY ASKED QUESTIONS ABOUT THE KETOGENIC DIET 48
    [HOW CAN I TELL IF I'M IN KETOSIS?] 48
    [HOW MANY POUNDS CAN YOU LOSE IN A WEEK AT MOST?] 49
    HOW MUCH CAN YOU LOSE IN ONE NIGHT? 49

Introduction

The ketogenic diet also known as KETO DIET is a low carbohydrate diet that promises fast weight loss. The diet is based on a biochemical principle that regulates the functioning of our body: ketosis.

It is a drastic diet that must be observed and dictated only by specialized doctors. It is not a DO-IT-YOURSELF DIET because it modifies the processes of our organism. The diet is usually carried out for 21 days and a break period follows. Let's find out all about the keto diet, how it works, if it works and what are the contraindications.

What Is The Ketogenic Diet

This diet regime involves the drastic reduction of carbohydrates and the increase of proteins and fats.

This diet is usually used to lose weight, but we highlight that it is not a DIY diet that anyone can follow, it is a difficult diet to follow and must be followed by a specialist for it to work.

Ketosis

Ketogenic diet means in fact diet that produces ketone body.

The ketogenic diet is based on the drastic reduction of carbohydrates in the diet: but why? Carbohydrates are the energy source of cells to carry out any activity. If this energy is lacking, the body needs to find a substitute: with this diet it will be pushed to use fats as an energy source.

This process is called ketosis and leads to the formation of molecules called ketone bodies: ketosis is reached after a couple of days of restrictive diet with only 20-50 grams of carbohydrates consumed per day.

In order to perform all daily activities, our body metabolizes glycides, such as carbohydrates and sugar, which are found in the blood. If we suddenly deprive the body of these two elements, it will look for them in its own stocks present in the body in the form of fats.

Ketosis is then induced, the mechanism that prompts the body to burn its fat stores because it can no longer find carbohydrates and sugar.

Reaching ketosis and keeping it unaltered without causing damage is not easy and must be followed by a doctor.

Are we in ketosis? the first symptoms

After a couple of days ketosis should begin.

To understand that the body has entered into the state of ketosis you can perform a urine test with special strips or blood test using blood ketone meters or breathing by measuring the amount of ketones in the breath.

There are also some clear signs that may reveal to be in ketosis:

exhaustion

dry mouth and feeling of thirst

increased diuresis

acetonic breath or sweat due to the presence of acetone

reduced appetite

Various low carb diets

The ketogenic diet is mainly used to eliminate extra kilos: it only affects the fat mass and can achieve good results in a short time.

The keto diet has different methods that can be distinguished in :

hyperproteic ketogenic or Atkins diet;
normoproteic ketogenic or VLCKD diet used in cases of obesity
ketogenic normo-hypoproteic which is used not to lose weight but for the treatment of drug-resistant epilepsy

Keto

Ketogenic diet: how to reach ketosis

The ketogenic diet is a nutritional scheme that can be summarized as follows
low in calories
low percentage and absolute content of carbohydrates (low carb diet)
high percentage content of proteins
high percentage content of lipids
In order for the keto diet to work we must first induce ketosis: how?
The first step is to eliminate from the daily diet sources of carbohydrates, such as bread, pasta, potatoes and sugar products, but also dairy products, legumes, fruits and vegetables of orange and red color.
Only meat, eggs and fish are allowed in the ketogenic diet. Food supplements based on vitamins and Omega 3 can be added.
It is fundamental to drink a lot of water, at least two liters a day.
The classic food pyramid is completely overturned! Many proteins, few cereals and tubers.

Only by respecting the dietary regime imposed by the dietician can you reach ketosis: you can never deviate because it would be enough, for example, a candy to bring the body back to the previous balance and stop consuming fat to produce energy.

Ketogenic diet: what to eat

The ketogenic diet is a low-calorie diet, low carb, zero sugar, high content of proteins and lipids.
What do we eat during our initial three weeks on the diet?
A guideline of the proper ketogenic diet includes an energy breakdown of:
10% from carbohydrates
15-25% from protein
70% or more from fats
It is recommended to include supplements in the diet as well, in order to make up for the lack of minerals, omega 3 and vitamins.
Let's see now what to eat in quantity, what to eat less and what to give up.

What to eat in quantity

In large quantities you can eat all proteins of animal origin such as
meat, eggs and fish.
cheese
fats and oils for seasoning

vegetables such as: salad, broccoli, zucchini, spinach, cardoon, cauliflower, fennel, squash blossoms, radicchio, celery, green peppers, radishes, turnip greens, ribs.
What to eat in moderate quantity

You can eat but in limited quantities and recommended by your doctor:

vegetables such as: tomatoes, pumpkin, artichokes, green beans, eggplants, red and yellow peppers, asparagus, leeks and onions
dried fruit, but to be consumed in small quantities.
fresh fruit only three times a week.

What not to eat

Avoid all cereals and cereal products such as
bread
breadsticks
crackers
sweets
pasta
Also to be avoided are: legumes, potatoes, fruit, sweet drinks, alcohol and foods that may include hidden sugars such as fruit juices, which contain 90% of added sugars and only 10% of pulp.

Beware also of sugars contained in candies, chewing gum, medications, supplements... just the accidental intake of sugars and ketosis stops: the body would go back to functioning as before and the effort made until then would be wasted.
An example diet for a week
Before starting such a diet, a professional should be contacted. It can be a very dangerous diet for our physique if not carried out under strict medical control.
With this diet regimen it is estimated the loss of 3 kilos per week.

A ketogenic diet is usually composed as follows

breakfast: two hard-boiled eggs with a side of sautéed vegetables or a slice of toast with cheese and avocado
lunch: a turkey burger with a side of cheese and avocado or salad with turkey, hard-boiled eggs, arugula, avocado, gorgonzola and croutons (30 grams)
snack: bananas, pineapple, apples, persimmons and mangoes in moderation or cheese
dinner: pork chops with a side of sautéed green beans or grilled salmon with a side of spinach

Ketogenic diet and physical activity

To accelerate and improve the process implemented with a low-calorie diet, it is always advisable to continue with an adequate physical activity. Even physical exercise must be recommended by a professional in order to achieve good results without weighing on a body that is already undergoing major changes.

It is generally recommended to train 3 times a week for at least 30-40 minutes: long walks at a steady pace, jogging in the open air, yoga or swimming practices are sufficient.

It should not be forgotten that doing sports during a period of high fatigue, such as it can be the beginning of a diet, helps because it frees the mind and reduces stress.

Contraindications of keto diet

There are conflicting opinions about the well-being that exercise can offer during a period of ketoacidosis. In fact, it is thought that sport can increase the weight of the ketogenic diet, which is however a metabolic forcing that already weighs on the body, even the youngest.

Be careful because intense physical exercise increases the energy requirements of glucose favoring the production and accumulation of ketone bodies.

Before engaging in sports activities, ask your dietician for advice first.

Ketogenic diet: Who can do it?

Being a rather stressful diet for the organism, it cannot be carried out for long periods of time and above all it is not suitable for everyone.

Who can follow a Keto diet? those who suffer from:

severe obesity;

mild obesity but complicated by type II diabetes, hypertension, dyslipidemia, metabolic syndrome, arthropathy

non-alcoholic hepatic steatosis

Who cannot follow the diet

The ketogenic diet cannot be recommended for those who

are pregnant or lactating

suffer from psychiatric and behavioral disorders

have type I diabetes

have had a myocardial infarction

suffer from liver and kidney failure

has alcohol and drug abuse

post-diet

Once the diet period recommended by the dietician is over, a couple of days of normal diet with the introduction of carbohydrates will be enough and ketosis will end quickly. The body quickly returns to function as before.
Usually for long-term maintenance carbohydrates are slowly reintroduced and alternate periods of ketosis with periods of non-ketosis.

Why it didn't work

Those trying the diet for the first time may not see results. Reaching ketosis is not immediate and it is not easy especially the first time.
Therefore, nutritional ketosis, the process that really burns fat and weight, is not always achieved.
What are the reasons for non-ketosis?
you still eat too much
you eat too little
you eat too much protein: keto is a moderate diet that aims at 20-25% of calories coming from proteins
you eat too many carbohydrates: you should consume 20-50 grams of net carbohydrates per day, not more

intolerance or allergy to some food. Sometimes food intolerances cause inflammation which in turn can lead to weight gain. While food allergies are serious things and we notice them almost immediately, food intolerances can be more insidious. Some of the most common food allergies include dairy, eggs, peanuts, tree nuts, wheat, soy, fish and shellfish.

Another reason the body does not go into ketosis may be resistance to leptin. Leptin is the hormone that alerts the brain that the body is satisfied with the meal, that you are full. It is therefore essential to be able to regulate the consumption of daily meals especially is essential during a low-calorie diet. If this hormone is not functioning well it is also difficult to communicate the sense of satiety to the brain and this can be the cause of unmotivated appetite.

Leptin resistance is often caused by irregular sleep, stress, overeating and caloric restriction. In the case of leptin resistance it may be necessary to wait before seeing even the slightest benefit related to the ketogenic diet, even eight weeks to start seeing results.

Ketogenic diet: contraindications

The ketogenic diet used against obesity almost always leads to excellent results in the loss of fat mass. It must be followed by a specialist, it is not a do-it-yourself diet.

It is in fact known that this diet has different contraindications. What are the main contraindications of the Keto diet:

ketosis is considered a toxic condition for the body: the disposal of ketone bodies above the normal amount can in fact cause a fatigue of the kidneys;

maintaining the state of ketosis during the whole treatment is really difficult. It is enough to ingest a single forbidden food to compromise the state of ketosis and push the body to draw energy from sugars

initially the weight loss is evident but it is very difficult to maintain the weight achieved. There is a high risk of regaining all the lost pounds when introducing carbohydrates again. Post dieting is really complex and foods must be reintroduced into one's diet gradually. The maintenance period must be followed by a dietician doctor

ketosis may cause discomfort such as nausea, reduced appetite, dizziness, headache, fatigue, difficulty in breathing, constipation, excessive diuresis, sweat and acetoxy breath

is a diet that cannot be followed for long periods of time because it is not completely balanced and would damage the health;

it may cause: hypoglycemia, hypercholesterolemia and hypotension. Therefore, the patient must be controlled by a doctor.

remember: avoid do-it-yourself diets. if you intend to follow any diet, not only the keto diet, always consult your doctor and a nutritionist, so that they can provide you with tailored advice.

KETO CRESCENT DOGS

Perfect for game day, Keto Crescent Dogs are family-friendly, incredibly delicious and loaded with fat. Think of them as indoor, keto-style pigs. Create a delicious dough with mozzarella cheese, cream cheese, eggs and almond flour. Cut the dough into strips and wrap each strip around one of your beef hot dogs. Place them in the oven for 20-30 minutes and take them out just before opening the kickoff for a fantastic lunch.

REAL TEXAS CHILI

If you're looking forward to some spicy chili, this mouthwatering keto-adapted version of True Texas Chili will have you begging for more. The dish pairs 100% grass-fed beef with onions, red and green peppers, and beef broth, and includes rich spices like cilantro, paprika, and chili powder. With a mixture of curly cauliflower and Oaxaca cheese, this chili takes the taste to a whole new level. The best part about this dish, is that Ketoned Bodies will deliver it right to your door.

FRIED CABBAGE WITH CRISPY BACON

The quick prep and cooking time make Fried Cabbage with Crispy Bacon a fan favorite among all the keto lunch ideas we've collected. Simply cut the cabbage and bacon into small pieces, fry the bacon in a skillet, and then add the cabbage, butter, and seasoning, and voila! Healthy, quick and full of fat and flavor, this dish is sure to satisfy.

BEEF FA-KETO DISH

This meal is another Mexican dish that is simply loaded with flavor. Made with 100% grass-fed tri-tip beef, this meal also includes seasoned cauliflower rice, sautéed onions and peppers, and plenty of Mexican spices. With pico consisting of tomatoes, serrano peppers, cilantro, cumin, lime juice, and black pepper, the flavors of this dish jump out at you.

EASY KETO SWEDISH MEATBALLS

If you like those delicious meatballs at IKEA, then you'll love these. These Easy Keto Swedish Meatballs recipe is low-carb, gluten-free, and overflowing with fat. These meatballs are perfect for the whole family and are pretty easy to make at home. Mix ground pork and meatball

breadcrumbs, use finely grated zucchini to add texture to the meatballs. Roll them up and cook them on the stove in butter. Next, pour over a mixture of chicken broth, mustard and cream and simmer for 5 to 10 minutes. These meatballs go well with cauliflower rice.

Craving a sandwich, but don't want all the carbs that come with bread? Try a Keto BLT with Oopsie Bread . To make the Oopsie Bread, start by separating the egg yolks from the egg whites. Beat the egg whites with salt until very stiff. Add the cream cheese to the egg yolks. If you want, you can also add the psyllium seed husk and baking powder. Once the two mixtures are respectively mixed and ready, fold the egg whites into the yolk mixture. Bake 8 small Oopsies at a time. To make your BLT, fry up some bacon, cut up some heirloom tomatoes, fresh lettuce and basil. Spread a little mayo on the Oopsie bread, put the sandwich together and enjoy!

PULLED PORK WITH MANGO SAUCE

The pork is slow-cooked for more than 12 hours and the mango salsa consists of mango, red peppers, cilantro, lime, garlic and avocado oil. The meat and sauce sit on a bed of red and green cabbage mixed with bacon, and topped with Oaxaca cheese. If you're craving a delicious and vibrant tropical variation of pulled pork, this dish is definitely worth trying.

CAULIFLOWER CASSEROLE TWICE BAKED KETO

Cheese is the name of the game when it comes to this dish. This Twice Baked Cauliflower Casserole Keto is loaded with an array of decadent and fatty ingredients, including full-fat cream cheese, sour cream, Parmesan and cheddar cheese. Pair these wonderful ingredients with bacon and you'll go crazy. Incorporate garlic, green onions and whipping cream to make the dish even more heavenly.

KETO TUNA SALAD WITH HARD-BOILED EGGS

Fresh and delicious, this Keto Tuna Salad with Boiled Eggs is a great number to add to your arsenal of keto lunch ideas. Celery, shallots, tuna, lemon, mayonnaise and mustard are mixed with the tuna to make a zingy salad. Boiled eggs seasoned with pepper are also included on romaine lettuce. The whole thing is then drizzled with olive oil. It all makes for a quick, light and tasty keto meal.

STEAMED MUSSELS WITH PIRI PIRI

If you're looking for a dish with a Latin American flavor, this Steamed Mussels with Piri Piri recipe features a chimichurri-style sauce made with red onions, parsley, red wine vinegar, garlic, jalapeño, crushed red pepper and olive oil. Steam the mussels in white wine and water and top with Piri Piri sauce for a unique high-fat, low-carb meal.

CASHEWS AND BROCCOLI

Take your typical Chinese takeout to new keto friendly heights with 100% grass-fed beef, seasoned with sea salt, cilantro, paprika, turmeric and garlic. Along with broccoli florets and beef, this Cashew and Broccoli also includes bacon, cashew sauce, sherry vinegar, almonds and coconut. Someone from Ketoned Bodies is happy to deliver this dish to you as part of one of our easy keto meal plans.

LOW-CARB KETCHUP STEAK WITH BLUE CHEESE ONION CREAM SAUCE

A nice juicy steak is the perfect lunch option that will keep you full all day long. This low carb steak with blue cheese onion cream sauce will have your mouth watering throughout the cooking process. Cook some Ribeyes in butter until they are medium rare. Next, sauté some onions in a generous amount of butter. Reduce them to a simmer and pour in some heavy cream. Melt in some blue cheese. At serving time, pour a generous portion of the sauce over the steak.

Keto Dinner

Lemon and Sage Creamed Chicken

Given its low fat content and high protein levels, chicken isn't always the best choice for a keto diet. But with a little tweaking, you can make up the difference and create a succulent ketopollo dish that will keep the ketones gushing. Lemon and sage creamed chicken (from Mark's Daily Apple) is one such meal. Bone-in chicken thighs roasted in a sauce of cream, cinnamon, garlic, lemon and sage make a delicious dish that really delivers in the health-fat department. And, at only ~30 minutes prep time (plus 45 minutes cooking time), you won't have to rearrange your schedule to accommodate this keto-chicken recipe.

Fried salmon with asparagus

Some easy keto dinner recipes are easier than others, and this one in particular may be the easiest of them all. This quick keto fried salmon with asparagus recipe from Diet Doctor has just three ingredients: salmon, asparagus, and butter, all fried together in one pan. Of course, that doesn't mean you can't can build on the basic recipe; feel free to mix in other low-carb vegetables, and serve it all with garlic butter. The meal only takes about 10 minutes from start to finish (including cooking time), so keep the ingredients on hand and cook them when you need keto dinner ideas in a pinch.

Easy Stuffed Peppers

There are two sides to keeping carbs down: one is to avoid carbs in the first place, and the other is to increase your fiber intake. In simpler terms, fiber is something akin to an anti-carb, subtracting from total carbs. So, low carb, high fiber meals are certainly some of the best keto recipes you can get. With that in mind, check out this recipe for easy stuffed peppers from Keto Connect . Cut some poblano peppers lengthwise, fill them with some keto-friendly ingredients, and bake them in the oven for ~20 minutes, and you'll have an easy keto dinner recipe perfect for bringing down your net-carb count.

Keto Pizza Meatballs and Mushrooms

This is one of our favorites here at Keto Bodies - so much so that we now offer it as one of our products. This recipe was originally adapted from Maria Emmerich's 30-Day Keto Cleanse cookbook, available on Amazon in spiral bound, paperback or Kindle download. This Keto Pizza Meatballs and Mushrooms dish is flavorful and filling. Ingredients include 100% pasture-raised ground pork, mushrooms, onions, bell peppers, avocado oil, pasteurized eggs, red pepper flakes and organic garlic. And with 57 grams of fat, 21 grams of protein and only 7 grams of carbs, this meal is a keto dieter's dream come true.

Salmon with Pistachio Pesto

Wild salmon is perfect for the ketogenic diet - it's packed with vitamins and minerals, high in healthy fats, and moderately high in protein. And (as the best keto recipes tend to be) it's almost completely carb-free. This particular dish, Salmon with Pesto of

pistachio from Mark's Daily Apple The dairy-free, pistachio-rich pesto offers a hint of lemon and garlic, and is thick enough

to spread. You can add some salmon to the pan and then add the sauce, and you have a new take on traditional seafood. Alternatively, if salmon isn't your thing, you can use this pesto sauce on a variety of other meats and vegetables.

Another of Maria Emmerich's recipes that we've adapted here at Ketone Bodies , the Deconstructed Pork Egg-Roll is a worthy addition to our meal delivery menu. It's tasty. It's fun. And everything about egg rolls reworked in a way that's friendly. The all-organic egg roll filling contains pork, coconut oil, garlic, ginger, coconut oil, sea salt, chili flakes and a variety of delicious spices. It comes complete with a fresh kale blend and is keto's answer to those Chinese food cravings.

Best Keto Brownies

If the idea of a keto dinner has you stumped, wait until you try to find some keto desserts! The good news is that chocolate,
when done right, is a keto-friendly solution to the carb-shaped hole in your diet. That's why these Best Keto Brownies (from
Keto Connect) are so perfect. No sugar. Lots of butter. Three eggs. Unsweetened cocoa. What more could you want? With only 3 net carbs, you'll wonder how in the world this keto dessert tastes so good. And while brownies aren't dinner idea (per se), there's nothing stopping you from

incorporating these easy, delicious, sweet and
fudgy brownies into the
Keto Chicken BLT Salad

A good salad is a great way to go for easy keto
dinner recipes, and this keto chicken BLT salad
(from Diet Doctor) is as good as it gets. A classic
BLT sandwich may not be totally keto friendly,
but replace the bread with some leafy greens and
add some chicken thigh and garlic mayo, and
you're in keto town. The prep time for this
sandwich is around 15 minutes, so as long as you
have the ingredients ready and have access to a
pan (for the bacon and chicken), you don't have
to plan this meal too far in advance. Just be sure
to take precautions when handling raw chicken,
or substitute in some pre-cooked roast chicken.

Boneless pork chop and zucchini spears

A juicy pork chop paired with some low carb
veggies is enough to make almost any keto
dieter's mouth water. That's why Ketoned Bodies
has included this boneless pork chop and
Zucchini Spears dish as part of our keto delivery
 menu. The pork chop is 100% organic pasture-
raised boneless and comes with a spice rub
consisting of sea salt, paprika, cilantro, onion
powder, turmeric, garlic and black powder.
Perfectly grilled, with a flavorful char and a
succulent center, this pork chop meal includes

zucchini spears and crushed cauliflower as a side dish so you can enjoy some good fiber along with your fats and protein.

Meatloaf and red pepper glaze on the sides

Bread may be a keto no-no, but you can still enjoy a loaf - meatloaf ...that is. And when it comes to Mama Meatloaf and sides the meal with Ketoned Bodies' red pepper glaze, have fun on is exactly what you'll be doing. Combining 100% beef grass-fed with green peppers, eggs, onions, heavy cream and more, and topped with a delicious red pepper glaze, this meatloaf is a great way to celebrate dinner while hitting your macros. The broccoli and crushed cauliflower sides bring in some extra vitamins and fiber and help round out the whole experience.

Wonton Soup

If you think about it, the only thing keeping traditional wonton soups from fitting into the keto diet are the wonton wrappers; get rid of them, and you're in business. So that's exactly what this recipe from Mark's Daily Apple does. This delicious wonton soup recipe hollows out the carb-rich wraps and has you roll the ground pork filling right into little meatballs. Cook them in the recipe's chicken broth stock and serve them all together with raw baby spinach or baby bok choy. Feel free to add chopped green onions and chili oil if you want a little more kick.

Chicken Saltimbocca

For many people, Italian food and the ketogenic diet simply don't mix. But3
what these people need to remember is that Italian food is more than just pasta with carbs. Take this easy Saltimbocca Chicken recipe (from Keto Connect) for example. A combination of chicken, ham and spinach, this recipe offers Italian flavors without the Italian carbs. The end result is a mouthwatering, delicious meal that sticks you with only 1.3 grams of net carbs per serving. And, if the ingredients listed are too expensive, or if you want to add your own personal touch, this recipe is easy to adapt to any taste.

Chicken Jambalaya Sausage and Andouille

Rice is pretty high in carbs, so before you can enjoy traditional rice meals on the keto diet, you need to find something to replace it. Cauliflower rice makes this possible, and is the perfect ingredient to complement the Ketoned Bodies Chicken and Andouille Sausage Jambalaya. This "dirty rice" dish will have you cleaning up your plate. Blending pork sausage, chicken thighs, and chicken liver with a variety of spices and low carb vegetables, this cajun treat will have your taste buds fluttering on your back, but won't break your body out of ketosis.

Keto Asian Noodle Bowl

Just like pasta and rice, Asian noodles are some of the first things a keto dieter will have to learn to give up before becoming fully fat adapted. Miracle noodles change all that, offering an Asian-noodle substitute with zero net carbs. And now, with this recipe from Keto Connect You can use these noodles to create a Keto Asian Noodle Bowl with all the flavor and satisfaction of traditional ramen. Incorporating chicken, eggs, mushrooms, scallions, pink salt, and a delicious marinade, this noodle bowl will make you rethink Asian noodles. However, it does require a little more prep time than some of the other easy recipes on this list, so be sure to take that into account when planning your meals.

Keto Scramble with Sausage

Eggs are a dieter's best friend - they're high in fat, contain moderate protein, and are essentially carb-free. But what makes them such a boon is that they're also easy to adapt to many different dishes.

Scramble with sausage from Ketoned Bodies is one such meal. Scrambled eggs mixed with sausage, cheese, red peppers, and more make a flavorful and filling meal perfect for breakfast or dinner. And, if you decide to create your own variation, you can easily add other low carb vegetables and high fat meats. All you need are some organic eggs, a pan and some of your other favorite keto ingredients.

Snak Keto

when you want to lose weight, usually the first foods to be eliminated are carbohydrates. in fact, a balanced diet should never be devoid of any nutrient, because they are all essential for our health and well-being. but we know that abusing carbohydrates leads to a rise in the glycemic index that certainly does not help you lose weight, so it is important to know how to combine foods for a healthy diet.

to dishes rich in whole carbohydrates, it is necessary to combine low carb snacks in the mid-morning and in the afternoon, to break the hunger and avoid binge eating during meals.

snacks, which, as mentioned, should never be missing from a healthy and balanced diet, are good, quick and give us an immediate sense of satiety. you can focus on snacks without carbohydrates: an excellent source of protein and fiber, vitamins and minerals and, perhaps during the heat and the summer, also rich in water.

Good and bad carbohydrates: what they are and how to choose them

But which are those that have a low carbohydrate content and allow us to eat without getting fat?

Fresh fruit in season

Apples, bananas, strawberries, oranges, tangerines, peaches or apricots are perfect for your low carb snack. Remember to prefer the raw version with the peel to store all the available nutrients.

Centrifuged drinks

To these natural drinks made from fruits and vegetables, you can add half a glass of semi-skimmed milk for a higher protein intake.

Dried Fruits

Walnuts, almonds, hazelnuts and pistachios as well as being excellent snacks (please do not exceed 30-35 grams), are an excellent source of antioxidants, vitamins and minerals.

Yogurt

Natural, low-fat, with fresh fruit or pieces, or accompanied by 30 grams of cereals, yogurt is one of the best low carb snacks!

Vegetables

Vegetables are a good alternative to fruit, as they provide a good supply of fiber, vitamins and antioxidants with very few calories. Try mixing sweet veggies like carrots, squash, arugula, radicchio, radishes, beets, celery and cucumbers, add a pinch of ginger and you're done.

Wheat, oats, and rye can be a great low carb snack, but instead of buying pre-made bars at the grocery store, why not try making your own? It's super easy!

21 Days Plan

The ketogenic diet, also known as the 21-day diet, is a dietary regimen almost devoid of carbohydrates (intake less than 5%) that triggers the so-called ketosis. This is a particular metabolic state in which the body, not having carbohydrates available, is forced to burn fats for energy production. By doing so, weight loss is accelerated in a short time.

During a ketogenic diet it is necessary to drastically reduce the intake of carbohydrates, almost to the point of elimination (less than 5%); on the contrary, an abundant intake of fats is preferred. In the field of nutrition, this translates into some precise types of food.

THE KETOGENIC DIET: A SCIENTIFIC APPROACH

The ketogenic diet is a dietary regimen in which there is a drastic reduction of carbohydrates in favor of proteins and fats. This operation induces in the body the formation of acid substances called ketone bodies, such as beta-hydroxybutyrate, acetic acid and acetone. The production of ketone bodies occurs physiologically in conditions, for example, of fasting.

Normally the cells in fact need glucose for their regular functions, but if the supply of the latter is reduced to excessively low levels, they will begin to activate compensation mechanisms, with reduction of insulin and activation of catabolic processes.

After a couple of days of fasting, in fact, there is a depletion of glycogen stores with a consequent stimulus to gluconeogenesis and ketogenesis, which will lead to the formation of ketone bodies usable by the brain.

Therefore, the cells, in particular the nervous ones, will use these substances as a primary source of energy. This metabolic state is called "nutritional ketosis", and is considered a fairly safe state, since ketone bodies are produced in small concentrations without significant alterations in blood pH.

It differs greatly from ketoacidosis, a life-threatening condition in which ketone bodies are produced in extremely higher concentrations, altering blood pH and thus causing acidosis.

Typically ketosis is reached after a couple of days with a daily carbohydrate intake of about 20-50 grams, but these amounts may vary on an individual basis.

FOR WHOM THE KETOGENIC DIET IS INDICATED

Severe or complicated obesity (hypertension, type 2 diabetes, dyslipidemia, OSAS, metabolic syndrome, osteopathy or severe arthropathy)
Severe obesity with indication for bariatric surgery (in the pre-operative period)
Patients with indication for rapid weight loss due to severe comorbidities

Non-alcoholic fatty liver disease (NAFLD)
Drug-resistant epilepsy.

CONTRA-INDICATIONS OF KETOGENICS

Pregnancy and lactation
Positive history of mental and behavioral
disorders, alcohol and other substance abuse
Hepatic or renal failure
Type 1 diabetes
Porphyria, unstable angina, recent AMI.

EVIDENCE SUPPORTING THE KETOGENIC DIET

(by the Faculty of Pharmacy, University Federico
II of Naples)
Carbohydrates now represent about 55% of the
typical diet, but it is known that a high intake of
sugars is associated with an increase in the
prevalence of obesity and metabolic syndrome, as
well as an increased risk of developing diabetes
mellitus. Recent studies in the literature have
compared the long-term effects of dietary
interventions on weight loss, showing no strong
evidence to recommend low-fat diets. In fact,
reduced carbohydrate diets have been shown to
achieve significantly greater weight loss than the
former. In addition, individuals following a
ketogenic diet initially experience rapid weight
loss of up to 5 kg in 2 weeks or less, which is why
we often hear the term "10-day or 21-day diet".

This dietary regimen also has a diuretic effect, reducing the sense of hunger and it is interesting to note how it often determines a saving in the use of muscle protein mass for energy purposes.

Fish, preferably wild (anchovies, swordfish, squid, octopus, cuttlefish, sea bream, sea bass, shrimp, cod, salmon);
Quality meat (chicken, veal, turkey, rabbit, beef);
Eggs, prepared in any manner;
Green leafy vegetables and Vegetables (asparagus, mushrooms, cabbage, chicory, spinach, zucchini, fennel, cucumber, eggplant, artichokes);
Fatty cheeses and dairy products;
Cold cuts;
Liquids: still water, coffee and unsweetened herbal teas, broth;
Snacks: fennel, pure licorice, take dima10g as a snack (in this case dose from a single scoop)
Condiment: 30ml of oil daily, salt without exceeding, apple cider vinegar (but not white vinegar/balsamic vinegar).

There is also a group of foods to be consumed only in moderation:
Certain vegetables (tomatoes, peppers, garlic, onion, eggplant);
Certain fruits (mainly red fruits and lemon), to be consumed no more than 3 times a week;
Rye bread;
Dried fruits, nuts, almonds;
Some beverages such as tea and coffee.

On the other hand, there are several foods that cannot find any place in the ketogenic diet, so they should be avoided completely:
Bread, pizza, pasta, rice, corn, barley and all other products made from wheat flour or cereals;
Potatoes;
Legumes;
Sugar of any kind;
Foods containing added sugars and sugars (also avoid sugar-free candy);
Sugary drinks, fruit juices, beer, alcoholic beverages.

WEEKLY SCHEME KETOGENIC DIET (DIMA METHOD)

Here is a daily ketogenic diet menu to be followed with a protein supplement (such as dima10g). The cycle should last from 10 to 21 days.
Breakfast: 2 scoops of protein (dima) dissolved in 200ml of water (or in 200ml of skimmed zero fat milk or in white Greek yogurt) + bitter coffee (or bitter tea);
Lunch: 2 scoops of protein (dima) in water;
Snack: fennel or pure licorice or Dima 10g (one scoop);
Dinner: chicken thighs and artichokes (or sea bass and beets or two eggs and broccoli baresi or steak and green salad).

The following is an example of a food menu to be applied as a first reintegration for 15 days, that is, after finishing the first ketogenic cycle.

Breakfast: 200 ml of skimmed milk without sugar, or low-fat yogurt, or orange juice;

Mid-morning snack: 1 low-fat yogurt;

Lunch: 50/70g of spelt or brown rice with vegetables 1 portion of vegetables at will

Snack: 1 protein bar (such as Dimabar)

Dinner: 200/300g of white meat roasted eggplant or zucchini.

Here is an example of a day's food to be applied as a stabilization for 15 days, or after several ketogenic cycles completed and in anticipation of a longer stabilization before following others.

Breakfast: 200 ml of skimmed milk, or yogurt 200 g, orange juice;

Mid-morning snack: 200g of fruit;

Lunch: 100g bresaola 50g whole wheat bread 200g vegetables;

Snack: protein snack bar (Dimabar);

Dinner: 200/300g lean roasted meat 200/300g roasted mushrooms

Here is an example of a food day of 1300 kcal based on a ketogenic regime, recommended for 7 days after a stabilization phase and in anticipation of a resumption of the ketogenic cycle:

Breakfast: 1 pot of white Greek yogurt (125 g) + 50 g of ham with 1 slice of rye bread;

Mid-morning snack: dried fruit 30 g;

Lunch: fish or lean meat (200 g) with a side of vegetables (150 g) seasoned with EVO oil (15 g) + Whole wheat bread 30g
Snack: fennel or pure licorice or Dima 10g (one scoop);
Dinner: omelette of 2 eggs + vegetable side dish (150g) + EVO oil 15g + a small fruit.

THE PHASES OF THE KETOGENIC DIET

We can simplify the ketogenic diet into 4 main phases:
carbohydrate deprivation
onset of ketosis
acceleration of weight loss and production of ketone bodies
elimination of ketone bodies through diuresis
In phase 1) the deprivation of carbohydrates is started by following the diet we have talked about.
The diet (also facilitated by the use of supplements, see below) will induce the organism to a state of ketosis in the first 3-4 days (phase 2). During this period the organism is stressed and may experience drops in energy, fatigue and exhaustion. If this occurs, it is advisable to remain under the control of your doctor and nutritionist of confidence, so that you can take advantage of an energy vitamin complex.
Phase 3) At this point comes the best part: the body is burning fats as a source of energy and in this way there is an acceleration of the slimming

process, which involves critical points, such as the belly, thighs, arms and hips (phase 3). The output of ketosis is the production of ketone bodies, which must be biodegraded by the body.

In phase 4) we have the elimination of ketone bodies through urine. It is advisable from the beginning of the diet to use a specific draining supplement.

FREQUENTLY ASKED QUESTIONS ABOUT THE KETOGENIC DIET

[HOW MUCH CAN YOU LOSE IN 10 DAYS]
The first tip with the ketogenic diet is not to look at the scale in the first 10 days. This is a method that tends to "deflate" hard-to-reach parts of the body, and this is regardless of weight. Also to answer the question we have patients who have lost as much as 7-10kg with the first 21 day ketogenic cycle. The subjective matebolism can vary the results, but we can conclude that with the ketogenic cycle you lose from 4kg to 10kg in about two weeks (10-21 days)

See testimonials and opinions of those who have followed the ketogenic cycle

WHEN IS KETOSIS REACHED?
Generally, ketosis is reached after 2-3 days with a daily amount of carbohydrates of about 20-50 grams. There is variability depending on the individual's metabolism.

[HOW CAN I TELL IF I'M IN KETOSIS?]

significant reduction in appetite;

dry mouth;

acetonic breath;

sense of fatigue (use a multivitamin to counterbalance).

[WHAT VEGETABLES CAN BE EATEN DURING THE KETOGENIC DIET?]

All green vegetables are allowed and can be eaten (except green beans), in the amounts provided. So asparagus, mushrooms, cabbage, chicory, spinach, zucchini, fennel, cucumber, eggplant, artichoke.

[HOW MANY POUNDS CAN YOU LOSE IN A WEEK AT MOST?]

If ketosis is induced properly, with a responsive metabolism, the body goes into ketosis after three days of carbohydrate deprivation. Therefore in the following 4-5 days it starts to burn fat as an energy source. When this circuit works properly we have verified an average loss of 2-4kg in the first week.

HOW MUCH CAN YOU LOSE IN ONE NIGHT?

Fast slimming, if approached in a rigorous and scientific way, allows you to lose weight in a week, in 10 days, in a month. Even reaching strategic areas of fat accumulation, such as the hips, belly, face, which are usually difficult to "sculpt". But slimming in one night does not fall into this category and is unlikely to bring benefits whatever you do. In particular, the ketogenic diet requires a cycle of at least 10-21 days to produce positive effects.

For more info on fast slimming consult the mainstay article of our blog that continues numerous resources, diets, methods and tips to lose weight in a short time: How to lose weight fast

CPSIA information can be obtained
at www.ICGtesting.com
Printed in the USA
BVHW041639030621
608739BV00003B/924

9 781802 760699